# stained glass

## GEORGE MARZOCCHI

*A big, love-filled thank you to my wife and muse, Terry, who was the wind at my back in finishing this book that I started in 2008. Her faith and encouragement made me get in front of the laptop and write, write, write.*

*To our sons, Damien and Julian, who have always been my inspiration and have never disappointed.*

*To our dear friend Loria Parker, who introduced us to Stephanie Larkin at Red Penguin Publishing, who brought this project to life.*

# CONTENTS

# PROLOGUE

Hi. My name is Maxie and I'm a numbers guy. I could've worked on Wall Street with Goldman Sachs, Morgan Stanley, and J.P. Morgan, but they didn't pay enough for me. I was a math genius at twelve and went to prison at nineteen for check fraud and credit card scams. I guess I wasn't as smart as I thought. I got 8 years in the slammer and it wasn't white-collar prison like most guys. They made an example out of me.

Now, you're probably asking yourself, 8 years seems like a long time. Well, honestly, it would have been less than five if I didn't slug the arresting officer. I was a lot stronger back then. When I got out, I couldn't work in the finance racket. So I got mixed up with a guy named Dom, who introduced me to Richie DiNapoli, who introduced me to the wonderful world of organized crime. DiNapoli gave me a job managing his money and, oy vey, was he a tough boss!

I knew it was dirty money, but I needed a job and it paid better than Wall Street. I was skimming off the top and it helped pay the bills. At the age of thirty-two, I had a five-bedroom house on Long Island with a private dock, a couple of nice cars, and a small boat, if you call twenty-five feet small. But sometimes the best-laid plans, as they say, get messed up and that kinda happened to me.

# CHAPTER 1
# MEET THE FELLAS

Four men are sitting at a table in an old-fashioned espresso cafe—Little Italy style. They call it the "Social Club." The man at the head of the table is the boss. Coffee cups and Italian pastry are on the table, and on the wall is an old-school payphone—the kind you would see on every street corner in the city back in the day. The boss thinks calls made from this phone can't be traced. The phone rings and the boss says, "Hey Dom, get the phone."

Dom gets up and goes to the phone, "Yeah." The voice on the phone says, "Gimme Richie."

Dom covers the mouthpiece, looks over to the table and speaks to the boss. "It's that guy."

The boss says, "What guy, Dom?"

"You know, that spic."

The boss gets up and takes the phone from Dom. The boss speaks.

"Go ahead."

"I'm ready, are you?"

"Yeah, Tomorrow night at eight o'clock at that dump you hang out in. Be there."

"I'll be there. Make sure . . . "

The boss hangs up in the middle of the voice's sentence.

The boss is Richie DiNapoli. Richie is a real gangster, not a Hollywood stereotype wannabe. Made his bones during the cocaine wars in the 80s and 90s. He came up through the ranks with Dom partnering with cocaine dealers in Colombia. They sold to upscale clients, stockbrokers, celebrities, and millionaires in the Hamptons and Montauk. They amassed a fortune, all of it in offshore accounts. Richie has movie-star looks—black hair slicked back with dark eyes. He has a great fashion sense, and is very dangerous.

Dom is Richie's capo—stocky, looks like he lifted weights a long time ago. Not as well dressed as Richie, but he's trying. Dom makes sure Richie gets what he wants.

Maxie is Richie's consiglieri and accountant, and he looks the part. Meek and humble, he handles the family's finances. He's under a lot of pressure to make sure the numbers add up. When it comes to the family money, Richie is unforgiving.

The man at the end of the table is Primo. Primo cleans up after Richie - witnesses, informants, whatever. He wears black a lot. He has big hands that he uses as weapons when it comes time to do Richie's bidding.

The boss returns to the table and says to the men seated there, "Tomorrow night at 8. Maxie, I'll need 50 grand."

# CHAPTER 2

# A BIRTHDAY FLIGHT

A 1959 Cessna 170 is flying over Long Island. The plane is red and white and it contrasts sharply against the blue sky. The plane is being flown by a skilled pilot as it banks, climbs and dives. The pilot is looking left and right as he handles the controls. He's flying over the ocean and waves break on the shoreline. The plane banks and is now over land.

The radio in the plane comes alive. "Charlie Delta 472, this is Baltimore ATC. You're clear to land on runway 9 at Suffolk Airport. Do you read?"

"Confirm Baltimore ATC. I read you."

"Approach from Northwest #9, over."

The plane lands and taxis down the runway. At the end of the runway, it turns right and rolls toward a hangar. The engines sputter and go quiet with the propellers coming to a full stop. The pilot's door opens and Tom Hartford steps out. Tom was a sergeant with the Suffolk County PD, now retired. He flew medivac assist choppers called Pale Hawk helicopters in the Gulf War. They provided air cover for evacuations on the battlefield. He was awarded medals for bravery, including the Purple Heart. He always keeps himself in good shape. Blue eyes with graying hair, about 6'2." Flying was his passion ever since he can remember he's wanted to be a pilot.

A short black man with greasy coveralls and a Red Sox cap walks toward Tom. The man is Scott (Scottie) Harris. He owns the hangar. Wealthy people store their planes there and Scottie maintains them. As he gets closer to the plane, he stops and looks underneath. As he's looking, he says, "I don't think she's leaking anymore. How'd she feel?"

Tom answers, "No problem, she's handling well."

"That's good."

As Scottie and Tom are talking, mechanics are working on other planes. Scottie is distracted by the activity around him and he barks orders to his mechanics. "Billie, make sure you tighten up that manifold."

Billie shouts back, "You got it."

Tom walks around the plane making sure everything is okay. He returns to Scottie. "Scottie, I gotta go. I'm running late."

"What's the hurry? Hang out a while."

"I can't. I'm meeting some of the guys for drinks."

"Oh yeah, what's the occasion?"

"It's my birthday."

"Oh, shit. Happy Birthday."

"Hey, Scottie, why don't you come with me?"

"No, I can't. I gotta stay. I'm behind on repairs but go ahead. We'll grab a drink next time you come by." Scottie extends his hand and gives Tom a hearty handshake.

"Thanks, Scottie. I gotta go."

"Go ahead, I'll take care of the plane."

"I'll see you, Scottie. We'll get that drink soon." Tom leaves and walks to his car. In the background, Scottie is still barking orders to his mechanics.

Tom walks into O'Hanlon's Bar and Grill in Oceanview, Long Island. Once inside, he's greeted by cheers from the five men seated at the table. The men are all policemen and friends of Tom. One of the men is Bob Fuller. Bob is a close friend of Tom, even though they never worked together. The men have their bottles raised in a toast to Tom. Bob is giving the toast.

"Alright, guys. Let's toast to Tommy. One of the finest men I know. Happy Birthday, you old bastard." Laughter and then an off-key, alcohol-soaked version of Happy Birthday. Bob takes a sip from his bottle and talks to Tom. Bob is a big man, 6"3", 220 pounds, dark brown hair, and brown eyes. He's been a sergeant for many years. He and Tom have partnered on cases before. Bob liked to drink, sometimes too much. Bob asks, "How's the plane? Did you go flying today?"

"Yeah, it was beautiful."

"Shit, why didn't you tell me.

"I was, but I wasn't sure.'

"Wasn't sure about what."

"Wasn't sure  your heart can take it, you old bastard."

"Hey, Tommy, go fuck yourself."  The two men share a laugh and drink from their bottles.  Bob asks Tom, "Did you decide about the house?"

"No, not yet."

"What are you waiting for, Tommy?  It's been over two years."

"You're right."

"What about Eric?  What'd he say?"

"We don't talk about it."

"Hey, Tommy, do something for me."

"What."

"Give Eric a call and talk to him about it.  See how he feels."

"Yeah, good idea.  I'll call him."

"You hungry?"

"Starving."

"Good, cause we're going to Gallagher's on me, alright?"

"Holy shit, Bob. Did you hit the lottery or something?"

"Come here." Bob throws his arm around Tom's neck and kisses him on top of the head. The other men at the table clap and catcall. Bob is looking around the table and laughing. "Hey, fellas, one day I'm gonna marry this prick.

# CHAPTER 3

# WHAT HAPPENS IN VEGAS

The sun is setting in Las Vegas. A car is parked in a facility adjoining a 4-star hotel. A man sits inside waiting. He's Hispanic in his 30s, a manila envelope by his side. He's impatient and looks at his watch. He scans the facility to make sure he's alone. From the other side of the garage, a car with four men inside drives in and parks.

Two men exit the vehicle and walk towards the Hispanic man's car. With the envelope in hand, he also exits and approaches the men walking towards the middle of the garage. He pretends to adjust his jacket, but he's really feeling for the 9mm gun in the waistband of his pants. The men get closer and they're both Middle Eastern. One of the men is carrying a briefcase. He's large and muscular.

The men meet in the middle and there are no pleasantries exchanged. The man with the briefcase addresses the Hispanic man as "officer." The officer is Special Agent Rodriguez with the Las Vegas DEA. The large man asks, "Is everything in the envelope?"

The officer nods yes and he asks if the money in the briefcase. The large man nods yes, and they exchange the envelope for the briefcase. The large man asks, "Are these the only copies?"

The officer answers sarcastically, "Maybe." The large man is staring at the officer and he says, "the Ambassador bodes you no harm and wishes you a long and prosperous life." With that, the other men exit the car as the large man reaches for his gun. The officer gets off the first two shots and hits the man twice. He falls mortally wounded.

At that moment a car drives into the parking facility, the headlights distracting the men. The officer uses the opportunity to run to the elevator directly behind him. One of the men makes it to the elevator with him as the doors close behind them. Both men are in the elevator as it goes to the penthouse, fighting for their lives. The officer smashes the man in the face with the briefcase and blood comes from the man's mouth. The man is disoriented and he's flailing punches as the officer hits him again with the briefcase to the side of his head. The man recovers and takes a knife from his sleeve. He attacks the officer and the first thrust misses. The second is thwarted by the briefcase the officer uses as a shield. He's not so lucky as the third thrust penetrates his jacket and slices his upper arm. The next attempt to stab the officer fails as the briefcase smashes on the man's head and he loses consciousness. In the scuffle Rodriguez loses his gun.

The doors to the elevator open and the officer is on the penthouse floor. The wound is bleeding steadily and blood is running down his arm. He makes his way down the hall towards the exit door and he hears the ping of the elevator in front of him. He picks up the pace but the elevator opens and the other two Middle Eastern men step out and he's spotted. He finds an open door behind him that says Sky Jump, and he climbs the two floors to the top with the men in pursuit. He encounters a security guard who shouts, "Hey, you're not supposed to be up here."

The officer shows his badge and he tells the security guard, "I'm a cop. Give me your gun." The security guard reaches for his gun when the Middle Eastern man fires and hits the security guard in the shoulder. The guard returns fire and hits the Middle Eastern man, and he falls wounded. The other man comes out of the shadows and attacks the officer. The officer is slammed against a concrete wall, knocking the wind out of him. The man is punching the officer in his wound, and the officer fights back and digs his fingers into the man's eyes. The man screams as the officer head-butts him. He opens a gash on the man's nose that gushes blood.

The officer has his arm around the man's neck and he tightens his grip. The man punches the officer's wound several times causing the officer to loosen his choke hold. The men are rolling around on the floor. The officer is now on top and pounding the man's face. The man again punches the wound causing the officer to scream in pain and this allows the man to get on his feet. The men are now fighting close to the edge of Sky Jump, 800 feet in the air. The guard is able to fire a shot in the air, distracting the men.

The officer seizes the opportunity and he kicks the man in the chest and he goes over the edge. The officer tries to help the man back onto the platform, but the man slips out of his grasp and he falls to his death. In the background, sirens are getting closer. The officer goes to the security guard to check his wounds. "How are you doing, pal?"

"Who are you?" The officer doesn't answer and continues checking the guard's wound.

"You'll be okay. Help is on the way." The officer gestures to the Sky Jump control. "Do you know how this works?"

"Yeah, that's my day job."

"Lucky me."

The guard adds, "Hope you're not afraid of heights. You see that red lever? Push it up." The officer does it.

"Now push the two green buttons and get into the harness."

"I don't have time."

"Help me up and grab the harness." The officer helps the guard as the sounds of sirens get closer. "Get over there and grab the harness. Don't look down."

The officer grabs the harness and says, "Do it." The guard triggers the descent of the officer at 40 mph to the street. The officer walks away from the crowds and the lights of the emergency vehicles. A taxicab turns the corner and the officer flags it down. Once inside, he leans back in the seat and closes his eyes.

---

Tom calls his son, Eric. "Hello, dad."

"Hi, Eric. How's Atlanta treating you?"

"Great, I'm on my way home. How was your birthday?"

"Good. I had drinks with some of the guys. Bob Fuller was there. He took us to Gallagher's for dinner."

"Gallager's is nice. I'm thinking about coming up to see you. I'll let you know when. I owe you a birthday dinner."

"Eric, I want to ask you something."

"Go ahead, dad."

"How would you feel if I sold the house?"

There's a pause, then Eric says: "I think you should. We had some good times there. But you're alone now in a big house. Maybe you can find an apartment in the area."

"You're right, Eric. It's something I've been thinking about for a while. On the way back from the airport, I drove past this good-looking house on Meadow Lane. The house is on a dead-end and kind of secluded. It was beautifully landscaped. From the outside it looks like a pretty big house. There was an apartment that had a for rent sign in the window. I'm gonna stop in tomorrow."

"Great. Go see it. You got nothing to lose."

Tom laughs, "With my luck, the Addams Family lives there."

"Hell, if that's the case, I'll take it."

"I'll let you know how it goes with the apartment. Once I get settled in, take some time off and come up. We got some catching up to do."

"Okay, dad. Sounds like a plan. We'll talk soon. Bye."

# CHAPTER 4

# ANNA SANCHEZ

Tom arrives at the house the next morning. It's a beautiful restored Victorian on one acre of land. It's isolated from the heart of town. Tom rings the bell.

The apartment for rent sign is in the window. No one answers the bell. He waits a bit then rings again. The door opens just enough for the woman inside to look out. Tom introduces himself. "Hi, I'm Tom Hartford about the apartment."

The woman says, "Hi, can you wait a minute?" The door closes and Tom hears the chain being removed. The door opens and standing there is a beautiful Latin woman with long black hair, brown eyes, about 35 years old. She gives a first impression of being a classy lady. She's dressed casually in jeans and a white shirt. She extends her hand to greet Tom. "Sorry about that. I'm Anna Sanchez."

Tom takes her hand, being careful not to squeeze too hard. "I'm Tom Hartford. Nice to meet you."

"Come in, please." Tom walks into a large, beautifully decorated house with early Spanish-style furniture. Rugs and tapestries decorate the interior. Artwork and antiques are everywhere. Daylight filters in and beautiful plants are placed around the room. Tom exclaims, "This place is gorgeous."

"Thank you."

"Did you decorate it yourself?"

"Yes, well, not exactly. My husband did the construction and I did the decorating."

"It looks professional."

"Thanks, I studied interior design in Madrid, that's where I'm from. So, do you want to see the apartment?"

"Yeah, I'd love to."

"Wait here, I'll get the keys." Tom waits in the living room, admiring the antiques and the artwork. Anna returns with the keys. "Come with me." They go out the front door and up a set of stairs on the side of the house. Anna describes the apartment to Tom. "This is your private entrance. Everything inside is brand new. We painted it a light color, but you can change it if you like." Anna opens the door and they walk in. The interior is illuminated with daylight. Tom is impressed. "It's nice, lots of light."

"It's bright, it's a great place for plants. The kitchen and bathroom are brand new. There's an extra bedroom that we added. Would you like to see it?"

"No."

Anna is surprised and she asks, "No?"

"No, I mean I'll take it."

"Just like that, Mr. Hartford? Don't you want to talk about the rent and…" Tom interrupts, "How much could it be?"

"It's fifteen hundred dollars a month."

"That's fine. I guess you'll want one month's rent and a month's security."

"Yes, if that's not a problem."

"When can I move in?"

"It's ready now, so any time, I guess. Let's go downstairs. I'll make some coffee and we can discuss it."

"I don't know. I should—"

Anna interrupts, "I insist. Let's go downstairs." Tom and Anna are sitting in the dining room. Anna asks, "Are you married, will you be moving in with your wife?"

"No, my wife died a few years ago."

"I'm sorry to bring it up."

"It's okay, I've been living in the house alone and it can get a little overwhelming at times."

"I understand, where is the house?"

"Oak Street."

"Oak Street. It's a very nice area."

"Yeah, we loved it."

"Do you have children, Mr. Hartford?"

"Yeah, I have a son, Eric. He teaches in Atlanta."

"A teacher. I have lots of respect for teachers. What does he teach?"

"He teaches history, 6th-grade history." Tom asks, "What about you? Any kids?"

"No, no kids."

Tom is looking around. "Is that what you do for a living?"

"What?"

"Decorate houses."

Anna replies, "No, two nights a week I teach interior design at Long Island College."

"So, you're also a teacher."

"In a way, but not like your son. I teach people who have nothing else to do. Some take it seriously, but most don't."

Tom is looking at his watch, "Well, I better get going."

"I'll walk you out." Tom gets up and begins to talk to the door and Anna walks with him. "By the way, forget the security deposit. Just one month's rent will be fine."

"Are you sure? I thought we agreed."

"It's okay. Just give me a call when you're ready to move your stuff."

"I was thinking of bringing some stuff over this week."

"Okay, let me know which day. May I call you Tom?"

"Sure."

"Call me Anna." They reach the front door. Anna unlocks and opens it and extends her hand. "It was nice meeting you." Tom takes her hand and gives her a firm handshake. She responds by tightening her hand, also.

"I'll talk to you. Bye."

"Bye, Tom."

Tom turns to leave and Anna watches as he goes down the stairs and closes the door.

# CHAPTER 5

# ANTONIO SANCHEZ

Anna and her husband, Antonio Sanchez, are having dinner. Antonio is a large man, athletically built with black hair, dark eyes. He is quiet but tense and menacing. They eat together in silence. Anna seems to be looking for the courage to speak. She puts her fork down and drinks from her glass. Anna reluctantly speaks to Antonio. "The man I told you about came to look at the apartment this morning."

"Oh, yeah, what happened?"

"He's gonna take it."

Antonio is still eating and he says, "Did he give you any money?"

"No, not today. He said he's coming back . . ." Antonio interrupts her, "That's bullshit, Anna. He ain't coming back. They all say that."

"No, Antonio. He said he wants to start moving in this week. He was serious."

"So what did you tell him?"

"I told him it would be okay to . . . " Antonio interrupts again, "That's not what I'm talking about, Anna. What did you tell him?"

"About what? What do you want to know?"

Antonio is growing impatient. "I want to know about money, Anna. That's what I'm talking about."

"I told him the rent was fifteen hundred dollars." Antonio is agitated and says, "That's good. One month's rent and one month's security in advance. Right."

Anna says nervously, "No, I told him one month's rent." Antonio is angry and he asks, "What about the security?"

"I told him just the first month's rent, Antonio."

"What? Why would you do that? What the fuck, Anna? What's wrong with you? You pissed away fifteen hundred bucks just like that."

Anna is intimidated and she says, "Please calm down and listen to me. I felt bad for him. His wife died and he's alone . . ."

Antonio interrupts, "His wife died. So what, this is business. I want the money. When he calls, tell him you want it. You hear me?"

"I can't do that. I already told him . . ."

"I want that money, Anna, and you better get it. Fuck this, I'm out. I gotta meet some fucking wops." Antonio grabs his coat and heads out the door. The door slams loudly behind him.

# CHAPTER 6

## OCEANVIEW—A QUIET LITTLE HAMLET

Officer Rodriguez is reporting for work a few days after the incident on Sky Jump. He fast walks past his boss's office, hoping she doesn't notice. His boss is Sergeant Elizabeth McMahon. She's African American and has been with the Las Vegas DEA for 15 years. In those 15 years, she's been awarded numerous medals and citations. She's cracked major drug trafficking cases and has helped take thousands of pounds of drugs off the streets. She's known for her "take no prisoners" approach to police work. This morning she's in an especially bad mood.

She sees him walk past and shouts, "Rodriguez, can you come in here?"

He enters and says, "Morning, Sarge." McMahon doesn't answer the greeting. On the desk are several folders. She insists, "Sit down, Rodriguez."

"You took a few days off, you feel better now?

"Sure thanks, what do you want to talk about?

"Have you been watching the news the last couple of days?"

"You mean that Sky Jump thing at the Stratosphere Hotel?"

"Yeah, that Stratosphere thing."

Rodriguez says, "What a shit show that was." McMahon sits back in her chair and stares at Rodriguez. She says, "I got a hit on my confidential phone this morning straight from the Nevada head-quarters of the DEA." Rodriguez says, "Damn, Sarge, you got a secret phone? I'm impressed."

"Cut the crap and pay attention, Detective." It seems the head of our division was impressed with the work you did earlier this year when you and your team broke that Reno meth distribution case. You took a lot of meth off the streets and locked up some big players. Well, it seems he's sending up the Bat Signal again. I'm sending you to New York, Rodriguez. Well, not the Big Apple exactly but a town in Long Island called Oceanview." Rodriguez is surprised by this news and he says, "Oceanview sounds like a fucking nursing home."

"Maybe so, but this town with a population of 10,000 people could become a major player in a drug trafficking case involving the Delacruz cartel.

"Delacruz? Shit, that's big. What does Delacruz want with a small town like Oceanwaves?"

"It's Oceanview, Rodriguez. Our agents south of the border are picking up some increased activity with Delacruz's cartel. Some of this activity involves the DiNapoli family in Brooklyn."

"Damn, two of the biggest crime families north or south of the border. What's going on, Sarge?"

"We suspect Delacruz wants to use DiNapoli's distribution network to sell a dangerously potent form of cocaine in this area." That's why you're going to Oceanview to look around and report back to me."

"But Sarge, I don't want to go to Oceanview."

"What I'm about to tell you may change your mind. Consider this transfer a favor."

"What are you talking about Sergeant?"

"I got an update yesterday from Captain Steiner." He's with Vegas P.D. and he said the guard that was shot can ID the guy who took Sky Jump to the ground. He said the guy flashed a badge and said he was a cop."

"Did the security guard get the guy's name?"

"No."

"So how did he know he was a cop? Anybody can say that."

McMahon sits quietly, letting Rodriguez speak, then she says, " I'll tell you why—because the man went back to make sure the guard's wounds weren't life-threatening. Only a cop would do that. He also said the man's left hand was covered in blood. Vegas PD found a gun that can't be traced and a briefcase stuffed with stacks of paper and on top of each stack was a hundred dollar bill. According to Captain Steiner it was about eighteen hundred bucks. It was made to look as if the case was loaded with money." "Those fuckers," Rodriguez says, surprised.

McMahon looks at Rodriguez and says, "Expecting more? Let me see your left arm."

Rodriguez sighs and looks up at the ceiling. "There's something else. Two of the guys were carrying State Department IDs from Kuwait. I think we're gonna be in the middle of an international incident soon."

"I don't know what the fuck you're involved in with these mooks, but for you, you're going to Oceanview. You'll be in Sergeant Bob Fuller's precinct. As far as anybody is concerned you're Detective Rodriguez with the Las Vegas P.D. Captain Steiner was your C.O. You were transferred because you're a disciplinary problem."

"Sarge, you hurt my feelings."

"Focus, Rodriguez, this is important. This is a joint effort with the Brooklyn organized crime unit. The guy in charge is Captain Danny Ebersole."

"When do I meet him?"

"Not yet. I'll let you know. As of right now, keep your eyes and ears open."

"Anybody, in particular, I should pay attention to?"

"Yeah, Antonio Sanchez. Introduce yourself, but don't make a mess."

"What's the story with Sanchez? You got any history on him?"

"Yeah, plenty. He started with the Delacruz family in its early days. He lived in California for a while doing odd jobs—you know, construction type of work. He went off the grid for a while and he showed up in Oceanview. He married a local woman and settled in. He was arrested a few times—mostly for fighting, the most serious arrest was for a serious beating he gave some guy once but the guy didn't press charges. He's had some drug arrests in Oceanview but he always manages to squirm out of it. Take a few days, Rodriguez, and read the file. Sergeant Fuller has your papers. All you need to do is show up."

Rodriguez says, "I'll be out by the end of the week."

"One more thing. I don't have to tell you these men are dangerous. We had an agent in Columbia who was able to smuggle a sample of this new cocaine to one of our chemists. It's true, Rodriguez. It's the strongest shit we've ever seen. We haven't heard from him since. Unfortunately, the agents we can trust are being frozen out by the corruption. We don't know who's on our side. Listen to me carefully. Don't trust anybody, including Fuller."

"Thanks, Sarge. I'll take your advice."

McMahon slides an envelope across her desk and she says, "Everything you need is in there, including your plane ticket. It's an open ticket. You can fly when you're ready. Sign the transfer papers and give them to Fuller when you get there."

"Thanks, Sarge." He gets up and heads for the door but he stops, turns back, and speaks to McMahon. "By the way, I almost forgot. These are for you," and he puts a set of keys in front of her.

"What's this?" She notices the name stamped into the keys: Las Vegas National Bank Number 37. "What's this about?"

"It's about a few nights ago. Those keys are for a safe deposit box and the contents will explain everything."

McMahon picks up the keys and says, "When this Delacruz thing is done, we're gonna talk about that night, Rodriguez. Remember, don't trust anybody."

Rodriguez says, "I'll be in touch," and closes the door behind him.

# CHAPTER 7

# THE TEST

I t's 8:00 PM in Oceanview, Long Island. A black town car drives down a dark, isolated street and parks in front of a rundown building. A large sign outside the building says, "Ball Breakers." It's a combination pool room and low-rent strip club. This is Antonio Sanchez's hangout. This is where he conducts his drug deals. He has a private room in the back where he has sex with strippers. He's the only one with a key. He's meeting DiNapoli here tonight in what could be the beginning of the biggest drug deal of his life.

Right now Antonio is doing coke with a stripper. The stripper is leaning on Antonio with her hand on his crotch. She's wearing a robe and stripping music plays in the background. She kisses and plays with his ear. Antonio says, "Not now, baby. I got some business to do."

"What kinda business?"

"Don't get fuckin' nosey. You get it—nosey? Here, take another hit." Antonio hands the stripper a straw. She takes a hit and laughs, rubbing her nose.

Richie, Dom and Primo walk into Ball Breakers. Dom is carrying a briefcase. Primo stands by the door looking over the room. The people in the room pause and look at them. They know it's Richie DiNapoli from the newspapers and television and they quickly return to what they were doing. Richie and Dom walk to the bar as they scan the room. Primo's eyes are moving between the door and the room. The bartender walks over. He pauses and looks at the men and asks, "What can I get you, gentlemen?"

Richie says, "Bourbon, no rocks and no watered-down shit, either." The bartender looks at Dom. "What about you?"

"Same. Gotta be top-shelf. What'ya got?" The bartender goes to the top shelf behind the bottles and comes out with a bottle of Knob Creek unopened. He holds the bottle up for the men to see. He says, "Is this good—brand new bottle."

Dom says, "Yeah, that's good." The bartender brings two glasses and he pours. As he's pouring, he looks at Richie and he asks, "Ain't you Richie DiNapoli?" Richie picks up the glass and without looking at the bartender, he takes a sip. He turns to the bartender with a cold stare. "No."

The bartender is no longer smiling; he knows it's Richie and he stands there not knowing what to do. Dom is looking at the bartender and he says, "You waitin' for a tip. Get the fuck out of here." The bartender scrambles to the other side of the bar. Richie looks at his watch, then looks at the dancer on the stage above him. He smiles and says to Dom, "I hope you wake up next to that tomorrow."

Dom looks at the dancer, tilts his head, and says, "I wouldn't mind."

"Come on, Dom. She's a crackhead, probably doing tricks in this joint ."

"In that case, the wedding's off." They both laugh and Richie says, "You're a class act, Dom."

Richie looks at his watch again and takes another sip. He's growing impatient. "He's late." He turns to Dom. "If this guy doesn't show, we're leaving. Fuck him. I'll let Primo talk to him." The back door opens and the stripper comes out and goes to the ladies' room. Antonio pokes his head out and motions to the men to come in. Richie looks at Primo and nods, and Primo nods back. As they walk to the back, Richie whispers to Dom, "Be ready. I don't trust this guy." Dom pulls a gun from under his coat and holds it to his side. The men enter the room and Antonio locks the door. Richie looks around the room and he sees cocaine residue and empty beer bottles on the table. He says sarcastically, "Is this a bad time, Sanchez?"

Antonio sees the gun at Dom's side and he gets nervous. He points to the gun. "What're you gonna do with that?"

Dom is glaring at Antonio. "I don't know. I was thinking maybe I'll shoot somebody." Antonio stands with his hands in front of him.

Richie looks at Dom. "Put it away."

"He kept me waiting."

"Put the fucking thing away."

Dom puts the gun in his coat pocket, still staring at Antonio. Richie adds, "Put the case on the table."

Dom does what Richie says. Richie turns the briefcase around so the lock is facing Antonio. Richie says, "Open it." Antonio opens the case and looks inside. The case contains rolls of bills bound together in stacks. Antonio says, "Fifty grand, right?" Richie nods and gestures towards the case. He says, "That's for you. Now gimme mine and hurry up. This place is making me itchy."

Antonio gets the message and clears the table. He goes to the back of the room to a row of lockers. He grabs a locker and pulls it to the side revealing a wall safe. He moves to shield the combination and opens the safe. He reaches in and pulls out two clear baggies filled with white powder. Dom has his testing kit out, ready to test the product. Antonio puts the bags on the table. Dom takes out a vial with clear liquid. Richie takes a small amount of coke and puts it into the vial. Slowly, the liquid turns purple. Dom holds it to the light and looks at Richie smiling and he says, "This shit is no joke."

Antonio smiles, "See, Richie, I told you it's good shit."

"The other bag—is it the same?"

"Yeah, Richie, it's the same stuff." Dom looks at Richie waiting for the word. Richie says, "Test it."

"Come on, Richie, don't you trust me?"

"No, I don't." While Dom does the next test, Richie looks around the room and notices roaches crawling on the walls and he checks his clothes. Dom tests the second bag with the same result.

"It's the same."

"Good. Take the money out of the briefcase, put the coke in the case, and let's get out of here before we catch a fucking disease." Dom does as he's told. Antonio extends his hand to Richie and he's ignored. The men turn to leave.

Antonio says, "Why don't you come by one night? We'll have a drink and I'll get you laid." Richie stops and says "Get this straight. We're not friends. This is business. Tell Delacruz I like his product. Let me know when he's ready." Dom and Richie turn to leave.

Antonio says, "Richie, can you close the door?"

"No problem." The men walk out, leaving the door open. Antonio stands there with the money still on the table. He mumbles, "Fucking grease balls."

Richie and Dom are heading for the door when Richie stops at the bar. He looks up at the dancers and one of them stands out. The dancer is the girl-next-door type, stunningly beautiful with auburn hair with long, flowing curls. She catches Richie's eye and returns his gaze. He yells for Dom, "Dom, come here and call Primo over." "Let's have a drink." The bartender walks over. "What can I get you, same as before?"

"Yeah, let's do it again."

"What are we drinking, Richie?"

"It's bourbon. Try it, Primo. You'll like it." Richie leans closer to Dom and asks, "What do you think about that shit? How many times can we cut it?"

"Two or three times and it's still better than most of the shit out there."

"Hey, Primo, what do you think of the bourbon? Pretty good, right?"

"Not bad, boss, but I prefer red wine."

"Hey, Primo, sometimes you gotta try something new."

Richie looks up at the girl-next-door type dancing above him and he says to Dom, "Check out that dancer."

"Nice piece of ass."

Richie calls over the bartender and he asks "What's her name?"

"Cinnamon."

"My favorite spice." Richie makes eye contact with her and she leans over and gets closer to him. He puts a fifty dollar bill in her G-string and whispers "What are you doing in a dump like this? You're too good for this place."

She replies, "Yeah, you too," and moves to the middle of the stage.

Primo says, "Hey, boss, I think she likes you." The men laugh and Richie motions to the bartender to come over. Richie gives the bartender a one hundred dollar bill wrapped around his business card and tells the bartender, "Do me a favor. Give her my card and keep the hundred, that's for you. If she tells me to go fuck myself, it is what it is."

"I don't think too many people tell you shit like that."

"You'd be surprised what people tell me. Don't worry, I'm not an asshole. I don't abuse women. No matter what happens, you keep the hundred bucks."

"Okay, I'll give her the card." Richie and the others leave the club.

Primo is driving Richie and Dom to Brooklyn. Richie asks, "Hey, Dom, who did she remind you of?" Dom thinks for a minute. "You know that movie with the masks where everybody's chanting some weird shit? She looks like the babe in that movie."

"You mean 'Eyes Wide Shut?'"

"Yeah. That's it, Primo. That was some kinky shit in that movie. Hey Richie, what's her name, you know the star?"

"Beats me. Ask Primo."

Primo answers, "Nicole Kidman."

Richie says, "Very good, Primo. Nice job. Must be the bourbon."

"Nah, I just like going to the movies. I watch a lot of them on TV and I like going to the aquarium, too". "That's where I go when you guys have meetings at the Social Club. My favorite is the Brooklyn Aquarium."

"Holy Shit, Primo lets his hair down. Surprise, surprise, the Brooklyn Aquarium. I would've never guessed."

# CHAPTER 8

# MOVING DAY

Sunlight is streaming into Anna's living room. Anna is relaxing on the couch reading a book. The phone rings. Anna puts the book down and picks it up. "Hello."

"Hi Anna, it's Tom. How are you?"

"Okay, Tom. It's a lovely day."

"Yes, it is. I'd like to bring some things over tomorrow."

"It's okay, Tom. What time?"

"Can I come over about ten?"

"It's fine. Ring my bell. I'll give you the keys."

"Okay, Anna. Thanks, I'll see you then. Bye."

The following morning, a moving truck stops in front of her house followed by Tom's car. Tom gets out and greets Anna. "Good morning."

"Hi, Tom, I see you're all set. Right on time."

"Yeah, these guys are gonna start bringing some stuff upstairs."

"Would you like some juice or coffee, Tom?"

"No, thanks. I'm good."

"Okay, let me get the keys. I'll change and give you a hand."

"No, it's okay. We can handle it. These guys are pros."

"Okay, then I'll make you lunch. How long will you be?"

"It's okay. You don't have to."

"It's my pleasure. You won't let me help, so I'll make lunch."

"Okay, if it's no bother. They told me about three hours."

"Okay, about one o'clock. Sandwiches ok?"

"Sure."

# CHAPTER 9

# DISPLAY OF BRAVADO

Antonio is in Ball Breakers playing pool. A waitress brings beers to the players. She's wearing a short skirt and tight top with black hair, and looks Italian in her late 20's. The waitress walks past Antonio and makes eye contact. Antonio nods and motions to the back. The waitress walks into the back room and closes the door. Antonio hands his pool cue to a guy sitting on the side waiting to play, saying, "Here, finish this for me."

The player circles the table, sizing up his shot. The player is Felix Reyes. He's twenty-six years old and a crack addict. Felix is 5' 4" tall with black hair and a thin goatee. Due to his lifestyle and drug addiction he's skinny with rotten teeth. He has no friends and he idolizes Antonio. Antonio has used Felix's addiction and his admiration for him to his advantage.

The waitress is sitting on the table with her legs crossed. She looks at Antonio as he enters. Antonio reaches into his pocket and pulls out a vial of white powder. He waves it in front of her face. He opens the vial and looks her up and down. "Stand up." She stands. "Take off your top." She takes off her top and she's not wearing a bra. Her breasts are firm and perfect. Antonio shows her the coke again. "You want some of this?"

"You know I do."

"You want some of this and I want some of you. Come over here and get up against the door." The waitress walks to the door and puts her back against it. He gets close and puts a small amount of coke on one of her breasts and snorts it off as she smiles. He puts some on a spoon and puts it under her nose while his hand slides up her thigh. She takes a hit of the coke and begins to writhe. He kisses her and she pulls away teasingly. He attempts to kiss her again and this time she returns the kiss. "You like that, baby?"

She takes more coke. "Yeah, I do."

"What do you want?"

"You, baby."

"Say it again, baby. I want to hear it again."

"Give it to me, Antonio."

"You want it now?"

"Yeah, do it now."

Antonio picks up her leg to make it easier to penetrate her. She moans as he enters her. She grabs him around the shoulders and holds onto his shirt. They begin a rhythm and with every stroke, her back hits the door with a steady boom-boom-boom.

Felix is still playing pool and he begins to hear the boom-boom on the door. He realizes it's the sound of Antonio and the waitress. He waves his arms to everyone. Felix shouts, "Yo, listen to this shit." Some players haven't stopped playing. Felix shouts again, pointing to the door. "Yo, bitches, stop playing and listen." The small crowd quiets down. All we hear is the music and the boom-boom and the waitress begins to moan loudly. The stripper on the stage continues to dance, oblivious to what's going on. Felix shouts again, "Yo, turn the music down." Antonio and the waitress are both into it and they're reaching the peak. The thrusts are stronger now. Felix says, "He's doing her real good." One of the players says, "No shit." Another says, "What the fuck is going on in there?" "What the fuck do you think? Keep playing, stupid, so I can beat your ass."

The noise coming from the back room stops and the men go back to playing. The music goes back up as Antonio exits the room. He walks out prancing like a rooster, smug and sure of himself. He knows they heard it and that was his plan. This guy can't get enough of himself. He walks past the pool table and looks at Felix. Felix looks at Antonio with a big grin. "Yo, you the man! You want your stick back?"

"No, I'm out of here." Antonio struts out of the bar and doesn't look back. The waitress comes out of the room wiping white residue from her nose. Everybody stops and stares. The waitress goes behind the bar, pours a double shot of vodka and drinks it down, slams the glass on the bar and looks at the men playing pool. Some of the men are gawking at her. She says angrily, "What the fuck are you looking at? Go back to your game, assholes." She goes to the ladies' room and slams the door.

## CHAPTER 10

## FINALLY WE MEET

The movers are finished and are gone for the day. Tom and Anna are sitting in Anna's dining room having lunch. Anna is talking about her family. "My father was a carpenter and eventually he started his own company and did very well. He died when I was young. Thanks to him, I was able to attend good schools in Spain."

"Your husband is also a carpenter, isn't he?"

"Well, he does a little bit of everything. He's very talented and he renovated your apartment."

"He is talented. The place looks great."

"So, you really like it?"

"I love it. I'm gonna move in next week."

"Do you have more stuff?"

"Yeah, the guys who were here today are gonna be back."

"Would you like another sandwich?"

"No, I'm okay. Thanks, Anna."

"You should get some plants for the apartment."

"I don't know. I'm not a plant kind of guy."

"Come on, they'll do well up there."

---

The door opens and in walks Antonio. Anna sees him and tenses in her chair. Antonio takes off his jacket, throws it on the sofa, and walks over to Anna. As he approaches, she sits upright in her chair, obviously tense, and Tom notices. Antonio leans over and kisses Anna on the lips and Anna does not react. He looks at Tom and says, "I'm Antonio, Anna's husband."

Tom stands and extends his hand. "Tom Hartford. I'm your new tenant."

Antonio sits down. "So, how was the move?"

"Okay, but I have more stuff to bring over."

Anna interrupts, "Antonio, do you want a sandwich?"

"Sure, baby."

"What do you want?"

"Whatever, it don't matter. You know what I like." He looks at Tom with a smug look on his face. "So, Tom, what do you do?"

"Nothing these days. I'm retired."

"From what?"

"I was a sergeant with Suffolk County P.D. I flew choppers for them."

"Oh, shit, a cop. How come you never arrested me?"

"There's still time, Antonio."

"You gotta catch me first." Both men laugh as Anna returns to the table with Antonio's sandwich and places it in front of him. The laughter stops and the two men are looking at each other suspiciously. Anna breaks the tension. "When did you retire, Tom?" she asks. "About four years ago." Antonio looks at Anna seemingly upset that she asked the question first. Tom says, "Anna tells me you do construction." "Yeah, when there's work. Right now, there ain't shit out there. Maybe I'll start selling drugs." Antonio pauses for effect, then he says, "Just kidding, Tom. Don't get excited."

Anna changes the subject. "Tom's son teaches sixth grade history in Atlanta." Antonio interrupts, "You think they care about what happened a hundred years ago? Nobody cares. All they want to do is play fucking video games and talk shit about the other kids in class." "Antonio, please." Antonio asks Tom sarcastically, "Hey, Tom, what do you think?"

"I think it's important. It affects how we live today."

"Trust me, Tom. They don't give a shit."

Tom looks at his watch, gets up, and says, "I gotta go." He looks at Antonio and says sarcastically, "Take care of yourself." He responds, "Yeah, see ya around." Anna comes around the table and walks Tom to the door. Antonio brings his sandwich to the couch. He throws himself down on the sofa and grabs the remote.

Anna and Tom reach the door, and she says, "I'm sorry for Antonio's behavior. Sometimes he can be rude."

Tom replies, "It's okay. Thanks for lunch. Bye." Anna closes the door and tries to walk past Antonio on her way upstairs. Anna says, "I'm going to take a bath." Antonio grabs Anna's hand and asks her, "What's going on?" Why're you upset?" Anna says, ``I don't want to talk about it." And she pulls away.

"So what's up? Why're you upset? You on the rag?"

"You wanna know why I'm upset? You could've been nicer to him."

"Why, he said something?"

"No, but you made him uncomfortable."

"Me? What did I say?"

"It's not what you say. It's your actions. I can't explain it."

"Well, Anna, if you can't explain it, I don't know what the fucking problem is."

"You don't understand. You were rude to him."

"I wasn't rude, I was honest. And don't forget he owes me money. I want the fucking money, Anna. Get it from your rich uncle if you have to. Just get me the fucking cash."

Anna is angry and she storms up the stairs. From downstairs, Antonio yells, "Did you ask him for the money?" Anna slams the bathroom door.

# CHAPTER 11
# INTERNATIONAL INCIDENT OR NOT

Sergeant McMahon is sitting at her desk reading the contents of the envelope that was in the safe deposit box at the Las Vegas National Bank. The documents reveal that the Kuwaiti Ambassador is selling weapons to terrorists. The documents also show that officials with the Turkish government are fellow conspirators.

McMahon puts the papers down on the desk. She walks to the door and motions to two men in suits sitting outside her office. The men enter and one of them closes the door. McMahon says, "Have a seat, gentlemen. Before we get involved in these papers, I just wanna say I'm not gonna tell you how I got the documents. I spoke to your boss at the State Department and she told me you were the best techs she had to authenticate these papers. If you don't think you can do it, let me know and I'll call her and tell her how disappointed I am. Take a look."

McMahon slides the envelope across the desk. The men open the envelope and thumb through the papers and glance at each other. "One of the men looks at McMahon and says, "these documents name names and places." Shit, if these are genuine there's going to be a lot of people going to prison including some of our guys."

They exchange the documents amongst themselves and one of the men says." It's going to take us some time to determine if these are real, is there some place we can study these in private?" "Is there an empty office we can use."

"Sure, there's one next door. But don't leave the building with 'em.

"So if these are authentic and the weapons were going to terrorists what happens then?"

"If it's for real, then we report back and the big boys get involved. You know - FBI, NSA and probably Homeland Security. When they get involved you're going to have to tell them where they came from. Do you want to tell us about it and save yourself a lot of bureaucratic bullshit?"

"No, I don't but I'm curious. Now that you've got 'em, what the fuck are you gonna do with 'em? Thank you gentlemen. I will leave you alone," and she closes the door.

# CHAPTER 12

# WHO IS THIS GUY?

Tom calls Bob Fuller and the Sergeant picks up. "Hi, Bob," Tom says.

"Hey, Tom, How's it going?"

"Good, can I come buy or are you busy?"

"Sure, come on. Grab a couple of coffees on your way."

"Tom walks into the precinct and is greeted by the officers on duty."

"Can we talk privately?"

"Sure, my office. Come on." The men enter the office and Bob gestures to Tom to sit down as he closes the door. "So, Tom, what's going on?"

"Antonio Sanchez. Do you know him?"

"Yeah, I know him. Did you have a run-in with him?"

"Kind of. I'm renting the upstairs apartment in his house."

"No shit. You finally made the move. Good for you, Tom. So I guess you met his wife, Anna."

"Sure, I met her."

"She's stunning, isn't she, Tom?"

"Certainly is."

"Antonio is a really jealous husband. He's obsessed with Anna. So, you wanna know about Sanchez? Let's see what we got. Hang on, let me get Detective Rodriguez in here. He's the new guy, transferred from Vegas. I think they wanted to move him out, discipline issues, at least that's what it said in his file. He hasn't been here that long, but so far he hasn't been a problem." Fuller gets up from his desk and opens the door. He pokes his head out and calls for Detective Rodriguez.

"On the way, Sarge." Rodriguez shows up at the door and enters the room. "What's up, Sergeant?" Fuller makes the introductions. "Detective Rodriquez, meet Tom Hartford. Tom's an old friend of mine. We go back at least 10 years."

"Did you work with Sergeant Fuller in this precinct?"

"No, I was with the eighteenth over on the north shore, but we worked cases together. Tom is a war hero from Desert Storm. Has the medals to prove it. Shit, he even flies his own plane. Yep, he's my hero."

Tom laughs. "Bob's my biggest fan."

"Hang out, Detective. We're looking at Antonio Sanchez's file. It seems Tom is living in his house—the lucky bastard." Fuller is punching information into a keyboard and he asks Tom, "How far back do you wanna go?"

"Whatever you got, Bob."

"Let's see. He lived in California about ten years ago. It seems he was involved with the Delacruz cartel in the early days. He was arrested in California three times for drug possession. Well, well—this is interesting..."

"What's that?"

"One of the arrests was for cocaine possession with intent to sell. Lots of cocaine. He was convicted and sentenced to eight years, but, get this, he only did ten months."

"Ten months—are you shitting me?"

"I kid you not."

"Sounds like friends in high places."

"No doubt, Tom. Maybe a politician or the prosecutor."

Rodriguez listens intently even though he's heard some of this from Sergeant McMahon.

"About five years ago, Sanchez showed up here. He's doing odd jobs, finally settles into construction, carpentry, and general contracting work. He's pretty talented from what I hear. He met Anna when she asked him to do some work in her house. They got married and he moved in."

"I saw the work he did in the house and he's good at what he does, real good."

"Anna owned the house for about three years, she lived with her mother until she died a few months after she bought the house. Supposedly she came from a wealthy family from Spain, I think. She studied interior decorating and was quite successful at it. She worked a lot in Manhattan redecorating lofts, brownstones—that sort of thing."

"That would explain the house."

"Yeah, I heard it's gorgeous inside."

Rodriguez questioned, "Was he ever in trouble here?"

"Oh yeah, he certainly was. I had a few, shall we say, differences of opinion with him. He's been arrested here mostly for drug offenses. There was one major arrest two years ago for assault, he beat somebody pretty bad, which could have turned into an attempted murder rap but the victim didn't press charges. We think he was intimidated by Sanchez and some of his asshole friends."

"What was that about, Bob?"

"Antonio and Anna were out one night at a dance club. A man asked Anna to dance. She accepted, which was ok, until Antonio felt that the man had his hands all over her. I would guess his jealous imagination got the best of him. It was probably innocent, but we're talking about a very jealous asshole. Well, that's about it, gentlemen."

Rodriguez asks, "Was Sanchez in California around 2009-2010?"

"Yeah, he was there at that time and he had some issues with the law."

"Wasn't that the time when he got busted and got out early?

"It was about that time, wasn't it, Sergeant?"

"Yep, he was there."

"Do you remember the cocaine wars around that time?

"It was pretty bad, dealers were killing each other and users were OD-ing all over the place."

Tom asks Rodriguez, "Do you think Sanchez was involved?"

Fuller answers, "He was there, but there was no connection to him."

"He has to be involved. He was in California at the time, then he came here."

"I'm with you, Tom, but there was never any evidence."

Rodriguez asks, "Does he have a favorite hangout?"

"Yeah it's a place called Ball Breakers. It's a dive, a combination pool room and strip joint down by the ocean."

Fuller says to Rodriguez, "Can you excuse us for a minute, Detective?"

"Nice meeting you, Tom." Rodriguez leaves the room.

Bob warns Tom. "Be careful around Sanchez. You just heard how jealous he is. He's fucking nuts."

It's a cloudy night in Oceanview, a mist covers the ground. Sanchez is driving home after a night at Ball Breakers. The drive is lonely along a strip of road bordered by the ocean on the right and the sand dunes on the left. The road is dark with no lights and no other cars in sight. As he drives, he struggles to stay awake. He has enough drugs and alcohol in his system to get him locked up. He notices a black sedan following close. Eventually, he hears the chirp and sees the unmistakable lights of a police car.

A tall figure exits the police car carrying a flashlight. His hand is on his gun. When he gets close enough, he shines the light into the car. He moves the light around the inside of the car checking the interior. He does this to deliberately aggravate the driver. He shines the light into the driver's face and motions for him to roll down the driver's side window. The driver complies and the officer says "License and registration." The officer continues to shine the light into the front seat.

The driver barks back, "Get that light out of my face."

"License and registration."

"Why'd you stop me?"

"I've been following you for about a quarter mile and I noticed you were swerving and driving erratically. One more time, give me your license and registration."

"Alright. Can you kill that light?"

"Not yet."

The driver lets out a groan and says "My license is in my pocket. I'm gonna reach for it. Don't get trigger happy."

"I won't as long as the only things in your hand are your license and registration.

He hands the papers to the officer. The officer takes them from him and reads the name 'Antonio Sanchez.' "Mr. Sanchez, where were you tonight?"

"I was at Ball Breakers. You heard of it?"

"Yeah, I heard of it—strippers and pool."

"You got that right."

The officer adds "and drugs."

"Don't know about that, Officer," answers Sanchez.

"Come on, Mr. Sanchez, we know what goes on in places like that."

Sanchez asks, "What's your name? Are you in Fuller's command?"

"My name is Rodriguez. How do you know Fuller?"

"Don't worry about it. You gonna give me a ticket or can I go?"

"Have you ever been arrested, Mr. Sanchez?"

Sanchez is surprised and he says "You can't ask me that."

Rodriguez hands the license and registration back to Sanchez.

"So that's it, I can go?"

Rodriguez replies "Not yet. I need you to do something for me."

"What do you want?"

"I wanna know what goes on in that shithole you hang out in. You know, drugs, hookers and underage girls stripping and don't tell me it doesn't happen."

"Fuck that! I don't have to tell you shit."

"You're right, you don't, but you stink of booze and weed and I get the feeling if we search the car, we'll find all kinds of illegal shit inside. Consider it a public service and a way to save your ass. I'll give you a pass this time. Think about what I said, next time I won't be so nice. I'll be in touch. Drive carefully."

Rodriguez turns and walks back to his car. The lights on his car continue to flash blue and white.

Rodriguez is driving back to town and his phone rings. The number is not familiar, but it's from Vegas so he answers it.

"Yeah" the voice on the other end says. "After one week, that's the best you can do?"

Rodriguez recognizes the voice and he asks "Hi Sarge, how're you doin'?"

McMahon responds "I'm here in the middle of a shitstorm. Those papers are real, and now I'm front page fucking news. Thanks, Rodriguez."

He asks "Who's phone is this? This ain't your number."

"I figured with all that's happening, I better use a different phone. So I went to evidence and got a phone that belonged to some mook doing time for murder in Nevada State Prison."

"I'm learning a lot of shit from you, Sarge."

"Save it, Rodriguez. You've got a lot of explaining to do when you get back to Vegas. I got people following me. Today it's this young agent, probably FBI, so right now I'm shopping."

"You're shopping?"

"Yep, I'm in my favorite mall. I know this place like the back of my hand. I lost the kid about half an hour ago. I'll catch up with him later. I think he's in Victoria's Secret."

McMahon says laughing, "So did you meet Sanchez yet?"

Rodriguez says "Yeah, about ten minutes ago."

"Oh shit, Rodriguez, tell me about it."

"I pulled him over for a DUI stop. I followed him from that dive Ball Breakers."

McMahon interrupts "What the fuck is Ball Breakers?"

Rodriguez responds "It's a combination strip club and pool room and who knows what else. I pulled him over and I told him that he was all over the road, which he wasn't. I shined the light at him and I knew he was stoned."

McMahon asks "You didn't arrest him, did you?"

"No, I let him go, but I told him to let me know when things go down at Ball Breakers."

"What did he say?"

"He was polite and basically told me to go fuck myself."

McMahon laughs, "Yeah, sounds about right. Listen, Rodriguez, you're not working this alone. I got an agent in Oceanview. For right now, I want you in the shadows. When, and if, the time is right, you'll meet. You're playing Sanchez just right. Keep at it, but don't scare him off. Be careful, Rodriguez. I'll take care of things here. Now, let me see if I can find that guy. Maybe I'll buy him a drink. He's kind of cute."

Laughing, McMahon disconnects.

# CHAPTER 13
## WAR HERO

Anna is setting the table for dinner.

Antonio is standing behind her and takes her wrist. Anna reacts and pulls away slightly but catches herself and looks at Antonio. He says "You know I love you, right?"

Anna pauses and says, "I know."

He asks "Are you thinking about leaving me?

"No, why are you asking me?"

"Cause I need you to be with me. Nobody's good enough for you. You know what I'm saying."

"Yes, Antonio."

Antonio has a menacing look on his face and it scares her. Antonio releases Anna's wrist and picks up his beer. Just then the phone rings.

"I got it. Fucking telemarketers." Antonio picks up the phone on the third ring.

"Yeah." The voice on the other end is Tom. "Hi Antonio. How's it going?"

"Oh Tom. Sorry, man. I thought it was somebody trying to sell me some shit."

Tom says, "It's ok. Actually I should be apologizing to you."

"Why?"

"The last time I was there, I forgot to bring the check for the rent."

Antonio speaks softly so Anna can't hear. "Oh yeah, the three thousand. Right."

Tom is confused. "I thought it was fifteen hundred. One month's rent.

"No, Anna made a mistake. It's rent + security. Three grand."

"Ok. I'll bring the check in the morning. It is what it is. I'm moving in tomorrow."

Antonio says, "That's cool, but can I get the security in cash?"

"Cash is ok, so you want fifteen hundred in cash and a check for the other fifteen hundred, right?"

"Yeah, that's right. Can you give it to me early cause I gotta go to work."

"What time?"

Antonio says "At seven, and do me a favor, don't tell Anna about the cash."

"Yeah, I got it. Seven's ok." Tom hangs up the phone angrily and says to himself, "What an asshole."

———

The next morning, Antonio is standing next to a pickup truck talking to the driver. Tom drives up and stops behind the pickup. He steps out of the car and Antonio walks toward him.

Antonio greets Tom, "What's up, Tom?"

"Not much. Here's the money." Tom reaches into the side pocket of his jacket and hands him the cash and the check. "I'll take the cash. Give the check to Anna if you see her today."

"There's a lot of twenties in there. I didn't have large bills."

Antonio takes the envelope and makes believe he's weighing it in his hand. He says, "That's cool. Money is money. Remember Tom, keep this cash thing between us, okay? You know, man to man."

"Yeah, no problem."

Antonio pats him on the shoulder and hops into the pickup. The truck leaves with the tires screeching. Tom watches it leave and heads towards the stairs leading to his apartment.

---

Anna is stepping out of the shower. We see her silhouette against the light coming through the bathroom window. She puts on a robe and walks to her bedroom and opens the blinds to let in the sunlight. A figure in the backyard catches her eye. She opens the blinds a little more, carefully so he doesn't see her. It's Tom dressed in sweatpants and an Army T-shirt. He's practicing Tai-Chi. Anna is impressed by his ability and concentration. Tom continues as Anna closes the blinds.

---

Anna and Antonio are sitting on the couch. Antonio is watching TV and Anna is reading a book.

Antonio asks, "Was Tom upstairs today?"

"I don't know."

"You didn't see him?"

"No Antonio, I didn't."

"He told me he was moving in today."

"When did he tell you?"

"Last night when he called."

"He called when?"

"You remember. Dinnertime."

"You didn't tell me."

"I guess I forgot."

"I guess. Why don't you call him and see if he's there?"

"Why Anna?"

"I don't know. I thought we'd invite him down. After all, we're neighbors."

Antonio is raising his voice and he tells Anna, "Oh, so now we gotta invite him every night cause we're neighbors? "

"I didn't say that."

"Anna, he's the tenant and I'm the landlord. That's the relationship."

"Ok Antonio. Let's leave it alone."

Antonio is getting angry. "You know what, Anna? I'm gonna invite him down cause you have been ignoring me. So, what the fuck, I'll talk to him. Where's his number—I'll call him now."

Anna is frustrated. "Do what you want. His number is on the fridge."

Antonio adds, "The Yankees are playing. Maybe he likes baseball."

Antonio goes to the phone and punches in the numbers as he reads them aloud. The phone rings and Tom answers.

"Hello."

Antonio returns the greeting. "Hey Tom. How's it going?"

"Ok. I have your check. I didn't see Anna today."

"Did you move in today?"

"Yeah, all the big furniture is in."

"Hey, Tom, you like baseball?

"Yeah."

"The Yankees are playing. Why don't you come down?"

"I'm a little busy right now…."

"Come down, we'll have a few beers."

"Ok. I'll be down in a minute. I'll bring your check."

Antonio hangs up the phone and returns to the couch. Anna says "Is he coming?"

"Yeah. We got beer?"

"Yeah, there's plenty, and there's snacks in the cabinet."

"Snacks, not for me. All I need is beer."

The doorbell rings and Anna goes to the door. "Hi, Tom. Come in."

"Thanks. Before I forget, here's the check."

Anna says, "Thanks" and walks to the dining room and puts the check on the table. She picks up some books and papers and says, "Excuse me. I have work to do for class." Anna goes upstairs, carrying her papers.

Antonio says to Tom, "Sit down. The game is on TV."

"Who's pitching?"

"I don't know. Some new guy. Are you getting used to living upstairs? Feeling good about it?"

"Yeah, I'm getting used to it."

"You can use the yard if you want."

"I know. Anna told me."

Antonio gets up and goes to the fridge and gets two beers. He returns to the sofa and hands a beer to Tom.

Tom says, "I was out there today."

The crowd roars as the Yankees score two runs.

"Antonio claps his hands and makes a big deal out of it. "Fucking Yankees! Yeah, go baby." He calms down and turns his attention to what Tom was saying.

"You said you were out in the backyard today."

"Yeah, I was. I was doing Tai-Chi."

"Isn't that some kind of martial art or something?"

"Kind of."

The door upstairs opens and Anna comes down the stairs. She enters the living room and sits on the sofa next to Antonio. He gets up and goes to the kitchen. Anna asks "What's the score?"

Antonio responds from the kitchen, "Two nothing. Where's those snacks, baby?"

Anna looks over to Antonio, "In front of you to the left."

Antonio returns to the couch next to Anna with the bag of snacks. "Tom told me he was in the yard today doin' What did you call it - Tai key?"

Tom says, "Tai Chi."

Antonio says, "Yeah, it's like a martial art."

Anna says, "I heard of it. Where'd you learn it?"

"In the Army."

Antonio asks, "Were you in Iraq?"

"Yeah, two years."

"Did you kill any of those assholes?"

"I did my duty."

Anna says, "Tom's got three medals."

Antonio looks at Anna, "Oh yeah? How do you know?"

Tom says, "I told her."

Antonio says, "No shit. You got 'em upstairs?"

"No. They're at my house. I'll bring them over this week."

Antonio asks, "How'd you get 'em?"

"It's not that important. I'd rather not talk about it."

"Come on, Tom. I don't know any war heroes. Anna wants to hear it, too. Right, Anna?"

Anna says, "It's up to Tom. I don't want to push it."

"Well, I want to hear it, Anna. Come on Tom. What'd you say?"

`Tom leans forward in his chair. He puts the bottle down on the table. Anna turns off the TV.

"In the Iraq war, I was a pilot on a medivac helicopter escort called the Pave Hawk. Our job was to provide cover while the Black Hawk hospital choppers picked up the wounded and the dying."

Antonio interrupts, "Those are the big ones, like in that movie, Apocalypse Now."

"Our gunner was a guy from Brooklyn named Rocco. In the chopper, we had a gunner, two pilots and one flight engineer. We had two fifty-caliber machine guns."

Antonio says, "Damn! Those'll cut a guy in half."

"That day, we were going to pick up four wounded. We were told the pickup zone was cool and there was no enemy in the area. We flew in with two Pave Hawks escorting the extraction ship. As we got closer, we spotted the smoke and the wounded."

Antonio asks, "What's smoke?"

"It's a smoke grenade that's used to pinpoint the landing zone."

We could see Rangers waving us in. I saw the stretchers and body bags."

Antonio says, "So you were cool. Nobody was shooting at you?"

Tom says, "That's what we thought. As we got closer, we took on heavy fire."

Tom pauses and takes a sip of beer. He looks at Anna, and she's sitting cross-legged on the sofa, her eyes focused on him.

Tom continues. "Our sister ship gets hit, but is still airborne. We're firing into the desert and the sand is being kicked up by chopper blades. My co-pilot is yelling for an air strike. We needed it to give us a chance to get into position to evacuate our men. In the first ten minutes, we lost three men on the ground. The remaining men on the ground start bringing the wounded closer to the Medivac chopper. I hear a thud and I see blood splatter the inside of the chopper. Billie Rudowski, one of my gunners, was dead. I knew there was no way those three men were gonna get those stretchers out of there without help. My corpsman in the Medivac chopper is taking fire from a sniper in a mound of sand. He radios his location and Rocco pounds the area with gunfire and takes him out.

Tom pauses and takes a sip of beer. Antonio is leaning forward on the sofa.

"Two men on the ground grab one of the stretchers and they get hit. That left only one man on the ground, Corporal Hernandez. I didn't think about it too long. I took off my harness and yelled to my co-pilot to get me closer to the ground. I hit the ground and ran to Hernandez. We grabbed the stretchers one by one and began loading the choppers. Rocco was laying down ground fire to cover us. Rocco contacts HQ to let them know we're coming in. We're still taking fire as we're loading the stretchers on to the Black Hawk." "A Ranger from the Black Hawk is giving us cover as we load up."

I turned to Rocco and I saw part of his head was shot away.The round came through the windscreen. He was twenty-six years old. I feel a sharp pain and my left arm goes numb. We get into the chopper after loading the last stretcher. "We get the chopper in the air and it's climbing slowly." "At this point we're an easy target, apparently the chopper suffered some damage affecting the rotors." "The next shot hits me in the leg.". "It came through the left side of the chopper." "I remember landing at base, then everything went black."

The room is silent. Antonio is staring at the floor. Anna says, "Excuse me" and goes into the bathroom.

Antonio asks, "Did those guys make it?"

Tom answers, "We lost seven men that day."

"You saved four of them!"

Tom says, "Like I said, I did my duty."

Antonio says, "That's what I'm talking about. Those fools I hang out with at the pool hall are suckers. They just talk a lot of shit. Blah, blah, blah. Not you, man. You walk the walk."

Anna returns to the living room.

Tom says, "I should go, it's late."

"When you bring the medals, can I see 'em?"

"Yeah, sure."

Tom rises and starts for the door. Antonio gets up and extends his hand. Tom looks at Antonio and shakes his hand. Anna asks, "Tom, can I walk you to the door?"

Antonio goes to the fridge and gets another beer. He sits on the couch and puts on the TV. Anna and Tom are standing by the door. Anna unlocks the door. She looks at Tom and says, "Thank you!"

"For what?"

"For allowing me to know a little more about you. Good night."

"Good night, Anna."

She closes the door and locks it. Anna walks to the couch and sits next to Antonio. Antonio says, "Wow, that was some crazy shit."

Anna doesn't hear Antonio. Her mind is on Tom. She's falling in love with him.

# CHAPTER 14

# THE NIGHTMARE

Tom is lying in bed, he's having difficulty sleeping. He hears the sounds of Antonio and Anna making love. He tries to sleep but can't, the sounds of passion playing in his head. The steady beat of the headboard hitting the wall and the sounds of Anna reaching climax and her cries of ecstasy are keeping him awake. The beat begins again and Tom sits up listening but the sounds have changed. They were no longer the sounds of love making, it was more aggressive and violent. He hears slapping sounds as if someone is being hit over and over. He gets off the bed and goes to the window to hear better. He hears breaking glass and Anna screaming. He lunges for the door barefoot and runs downstairs. He breaks through the front door and runs up to their bedroom. The slaps now sound like punches and the screams are low and muted. The bedroom door is open and Anna is lying on the bed. Antonio is beating her; her face is bloody. Tom lunges and grabs Antonio around the neck to pull him off Anna. Antonio fights him off and punches Tom in the face sending him against the wall. Tom retaliates and kicks Antonia in the chest that sends Antonio into the night stand. Anna is lying on the bed not moving. Tom lunges at Antonio again but this time he's grabbed from behind. Tom feels… strong arms around him pinning his arms at his side. The arms were not warm like human's but cold and icy. They were clad in a flight suit just like the one they wore in Iraq. Over his shoulder Tom could feel a cold chill. He struggles to turn to see who's behind him. He manages to break free and turns to face his attacker. It's Rocco, his gunner, half his head is missing and blood stains the right side of his flight suit. Tom wants to scream but he can't. Antonio and Rocco now come at Tom together. Antonio is laughing maniacally. Tom is backed into the wall. Rocco gets closer and reaches for Tom. Tom wakes up his heart pounding. His breathing is heavy and he feels as if he may hyperventilate. He puts on the light and looks around the room to make sure he's alone. He breathes more normally and sits on the edge of the bed for a while.

The next morning Tom awakens and opens the blinds to let in the sunlight.

---

The nightmare is now just a bad memory. He decides to take the plane for a flight and he calls Scottie. Scottie is sitting behind a desk in his office. The office is spacious but not organized. Airplane parts are stacked along one wall. Scottie's doing paperwork. A single window, large and gated, is behind him. His cell phone is on the desk and it rings "Scottie's." Tom says, "Good Morning, Scottie." Tom hears mechanics working on planes and it's noisy. Scottie is having a hard time hearing Tom. He walks to the door and closes it.

"Hey, Tom. How're you doing?"

"I'm alright. You want me to fuel her up?"

"I was thinking about Friday morning."

"Ok, Tom. I'll have her ready around ten."

"You got it. See you then."

# CHAPTER 15

# PAY DAY

It's a misty night in Oceanview; a black car is parked with the engine running. A street light bathes the scene with a soft glow. Another car comes alongside and stops. The driver's side window lowers and it's Dom. Primo is in the passenger seat and on the dashboard is a plastic bag. On the seat next to Dom is a gun. The man in the other car lowers the window. Dom says sarcastically, "Well if it ain't Sergeant Fuller. Lovely night, ain't it, Fuller?"

"Throw it in, Dom."

"What's up Fuller—no small talk this evening."

Fuller responds angrily, "Put it in the fucking car."

Dom takes the bag full of money and throws it into the open window of the car. Sergeant Fuller is staring straight ahead.

Dom says, "Good night, Fuller." Fuller's car window goes up and his car drives off and disappears around the corner. Dom and Primo are still in the same place as a soft rain continues to fall.

Dom says "I'd like to shoot that fuck right in the face."

"You can't. Richie said it's bad to kill a cop."

"I know what Richie said, Primo. I didn't say I was gonna do it."

"But Richie don't want the guy dead. He says never kill a cop."

"Primo, listen carefully. I'm not going to kill Fuller."

"Ok, Dom. I get it."

"Jesus Christ, Primo, do me a favor on the way back to Brooklyn. Don't say a fucking word."

"Hey, Dom. Why're you getting upset?" The window of the car goes up and it drives off. At the corner it makes a right.

# CHAPTER 16

# TOM'S HOUSE

Tom hears stirring on his porch. He opens the door and is startled, what he thought was a person standing there was actually a plant.

He brings the plant inside, smiling. He goes to his car and he sees Anna on her porch. Anna calls, "Hi, Tom. How are you?"

"I'm good, Anna."

"How's the apartment? Is everything ok?" Tom wasn't going to mention the plant yet. He was going to toy with her.

"Yep."

"So are you done with the boxes?"

"Not yet. There's a lot of years in those boxes."

"Are you bringing more today?"

"Yeah I'm going back for more now." As if on cue Anna opens the passenger door and jumps in. Tom pokes his head into the window and looks at Anna. "And where are you going?"

"With you, in case you need help."

"I'm ok."

"I insist. Besides if I don't help you, you'll be bringing boxes for the rest of the year. So come on. Let's go."

"Fine, but just one trip, ok."

"Ok Tom. Besides, I got some shopping to do."

Tom gets into the car, buckles up and starts the engine. He looks at Anna and she returns his gaze and smiles. Tom smiles back.

Anna is looking out the window and she asks "So, everything was ok upstairs?"

"What do you mean?"

Anna turns to Tom. "Nothing unusual with the apartment."

Tom says "Let me see. Well something did happen when I got upstairs. There was this big green thing in front of the door. Thanks for the plant."

Anna says with a confused look "What plant?"

They both laugh. Anna shifts her position and moves closer to Tom. Tom welcomes it and he can smell her perfume. The car drives and stops in front of Tom's house. Anna leans out of the window and looks at the house. Tom exits and comes around to open Anna's door. She steps out and continues to look at the house.

Anna says "I can see why you liked it. It's beautiful."

"Thanks, let go in." They go up the stairs. Tom unlocks the door and ushers Anna inside.

The interior looks like a house in the middle of a move. Furniture is in one corner, rugs are rolled up, and boxes are piled up in another corner. Anna looks around. "Looks like you're serious about this move."

"Yeah. You want something to drink?"

"No, not now, thanks."

"Come on, I'll show you around." Tom takes Anna to the living room. There's boxes piled up against the walls. Paintings are neatly placed in one area of the room. Anna admires the fireplace, then her attention shifts to the stained glass windows on one side of the house.

"I love the stained glass windows."

"Thanks, Rebecca did them. My wife."

"Wow, she did those?"

"Yeah she took some courses and practiced a lot. About six months and some broken glass later, that's the result. She got good at it eventually."

"They're fabulous and she learned quickly."

"Yeah, she was something else."

"I'm going to bring them to the apartment today and hang them in front of the living room windows."

"I love the fireplace."

On the fireplace are several pictures. They're pictures of Tom and his family. In the middle is a glass covered mahogany box standing upright. Inside the box on black velvet are 3 military medals. In the center of the three is the Purple Heart. Anna asks, "Are these the medals you told us about."

"Yes, they are." Also on the mantel are pictures of Tom's family. She picks up a framed picture with three people in it. It's a formal portrait with Tom in his police dress uniform. Anna asks, "Is this Rebecca and your son?"

"Yes it is."

"She's beautiful. Your whole family is."

"Thanks. Come on, I'll show you the kitchen. I think you'll like it." Tom and Anna walk to the kitchen. Anna is walking closer to Tom, her body language becoming more seductive. They reach the kitchen and her eyes light up.

"A country kitchen. I love it!"

"It was Rebecca's idea."

"It's wonderful, the whole house is. It feels like a real home with lots of love."

"Thanks. There was." Anna is sensing a change in Tom's mood.

"Maybe we should get back," Tom says. "Do you still wanna take a few boxes."

"Of course, that's why I came."

"They're over here, let's take six or seven."

"I don't think we can fit more than that in the car." Tom and Anna walk over to where the boxes are. They're piled up in a small room to the left of the empty dining room. Tom says "I'll take the heavy ones and you take the light ones."

"Why, don't you think I'm strong enough?"

Tom looks at Anna and smiles. He turns to pick up the top box on the pile. He grabs the box and turns to Anna, she is now standing directly in front of him. Again he gets a whiff of her sweet scent. Anna extends her arms as if to take the box. Anna asks, "Is it a light one or a heavy one?"

"Light one, it's yours."

She takes the box and her hand brushes against his. Tom asks "Think you can handle it?"

"Yeah I got it." Anna takes the box and walks toward the door. She turns to Tom and asks, "Are you coming?" Tom bends to pick up a box. He lets out a groan as he lifts it. Anna says, "Not too heavy, is it?" Tom says, "Shut up."

After the last box is loaded Anna sits in the passenger seat. Tom locks the door and comes down the stairs carrying two books. He hands them to Anna, she looks at the books, they're both about stained glass. Tom says "I thought you might find 'em interesting. Give 'em back when you're done."

"Thank you Tom, I'm gonna try it." They drive away.

---

Tom is hanging the stained glass frames in front of the living room windows.The light coming through them bathes the room in muted colors." The furniture is in place and Anna's plant is in the corner by the window. the doorbell rings and Tom opens the door. Anna is standing there holding a large plate covered in aluminum foil.

Tom is surprised to see Anna and he invites her in. "Hi Anna. Was I making too much noise?"

"No, not at all, I bought you some food. Chicken and rice, black beans and some salad." Tom takes the plate from Anna. "That's nice, Anna. I'll have it for dinner. Thank you." Tom walks into the kitchen and says, "Have a seat in the living room." Anna looks around at the artwork on the walls.

"I love your paintings. Are they from local artists?"

"Yeah, Rebecca insisted we support local artists. I have more at the house. I gotta bring them over." "The stained glass panels look beautiful."

"I see you hung up your medals. Good for you. You should be proud. The place looks nice. I see the plant is still alive."

Tom says laughing "I'm trying to, so far so good. Don't you have a class tonight."

"I do, but it's later on."

"How is it? Do you enjoy it?"

Anna responds, "It's alright, but the people are coming from work. They're tired, hungry and not very focused. I try to make it interesting."

"I'm sure you do."

"Tom, I didn't come up just to bring you food. I wanted to apologize for Antonio the other day. I know he makes you uncomfortable."

"It's ok. Already forgotten."

"I don't want you to avoid us because of Antonio. We're neighbors, we may need each other one day. The other night when you left all he talked about was you."

"Me?"

Anna says, "Yes, you. Antonio considers himself a very Macho guy. He thinks he's better than any man but you really impressed him."

"Because of the war?"

"Yes, and your medals. You're a tough man, Tom, but you have inner strength and confidence. You have nothing to prove to anybody. From the little time I've known you I see that you're a kind man. You don't need to be alone." Tom is feeling uncomfortable and he says "I have to get back to work."

Anna replies "It seems I've made you uncomfortable. I have to get ready for class." Anna stands and Tom walks her to the door. Anna looks at Tom and says "I'm sorry if I made you uneasy."

Tom says, "It's fine. I appreciate what you said. Bye Anna." Anna says, "Bye, Tom." She turns and goes down the stairs. Tom closes the door behind her.

# CHAPTER 17

# FELIX AND THE STRIPPER

Later that day Anna is cooking. As she cooks, she's reading one of the stained glass books. The door opens and it's Antonio. Antonio walks in, throws his coat on the couch and takes off his work boots. He walks to the kitchen and says, "Hi, baby. Shit, I'm tired." Antonio puts his arms around Anna's waist. He sniffs her hair and kisses her on the neck. Anna turns and acknowledges the kiss. Anna says "That was nice."

Antonio asks "You got class tonight."

"Yeah."

"What time are you coming back, baby?"

"I'm usually home by ten. Why're you asking, Antonio?"

"How about I stay home tonight and wait for you?"

What'd you got in mind?"

"You'll see when you get back, baby."

"Promise me you won't drink too much." You scare me when you drink. I don't enjoy being with you when you're drinking.

Antonio says, "But babe, I gotta have a couple."

"Please, Antonio." Antonio gives in. "Ok, I promise."

They're still hugging when Antonio notices the stained glass book. He lets go of Anna and walks over to where the book is. He asks, "What're you reading."

Anna says "It's a book about stained glass."

"Stained glass, like church windows."

"It's a book about how to put stained glass together. I was thinking of trying it."

"Oh yeah? Where did you get it?"

The question took Anna by surprise and put her off guard. She didn't think Antonio would care about the book. He never asked about her other books. She didn't want to tell him the truth, she knows how jealous he is. She hesitated, making believe she didn't hear the question. Antonio asks again "Where'd you get the book, Anna?"

"At the library, I picked it up today."

" So you're really going to try it."

"Yeah I think so. Sit down, dinner is ready."

---

Felix is playing pool in Ball Breakers. He's hustling somebody, stoned as usual. He's in the middle of the game when he's approached by Antonios's stripper girlfriend. She's in need of a hit and she's frantically searching for Antonio. She's wearing a red robe with just a G string underneath. She's scheduled to dance next. She stands next to Felix and says, "Felix, can I talk to you?"

"Yeah what's up? I'm in the middle of a game."

"Can you give me something?"

Felix says quietly, "Where's Antonio?"

"How the fuck do I know."

"What do you want?" Felix is paying attention to the game as he talks to her.

"Anything, it don't matter."

"Meet me in the ladies room. Give me 5 minutes to beat this chump." The stripper walks to the ladies room. Felix continues to play and runs the next 5 balls. If he sinks the next 3 balls he wins the game and takes 50 dollars from his opponent.

Felix states, "If I get these three in, you're done. I hope you got the money fifty bucks, right?" His opponent says, "I got it. Go ahead."

Felix makes the three shots and wins the game. Angrily the player reaches into his pocket and gives Felix fifty dollars. Felix peels the bills one at a time and counts out loud smugly. "Want a rematch?"

"No, that's ok." Felix hands the stick to the next player and walks to the bathroom. He opens the door and the stripper is leaning against the sink. The bathroom is small, and a single bulb hangs in the middle. A steam pipe with rust stains is in one corner. The sink has a leak and the toilet has no cover. The walls are painted a loud red and the room smells of urine and bleach. Felix reaches into his pocket and takes out a baggie with rocks of crack in it. He asks the stripper "You got a pipe?" She answers, "Yeah."

The stripper reaches into the pocket of her robe and takes out a pipe. She takes out a lighter and hands it to Felix. She puts the pipe to her lips. Felix gets the lighter ready. "You ready?" The stripper nods yes. Felix lights up the rock and she takes a slow deep drag and holds it. Her head goes back, her eyes half closed as she exhales. "Nice hit. Is it good?" She doesn't answer, she just looks at him with half closed eyes. She says "Hit me again."

"Sure, baby." The ritual is repeated. The stripper getting deeper into the high."

Felix asks "How do you feel?"

"Nice, aren't you gonna take a hit?"

"Not yet, you got some money for me?"

The stripper is a little surprised by the question and she looks at Felix.

"You know I got no money."

"Well, this shit ain't free."

"You didn't say shit about money, Felix."

"It don't have to be money." She says, "Sex. You want sex. Is that it?"

"You know I was always hot for that ass."

She says sleepily, "Can I have the other rock?"

"You gonna fuck me for it?" Felix asks.

"Yeah, but give me the rock first."

"No, after."

"Later. I'll fuck you later. Let's do the other rock."

Felix takes the pipe out of her hand and takes a hit himself. He takes a deep drag and lets out the smoke. He puts his hand around her neck, not squeezing just holding her in place. He gets in her face. She could smell his rotten teeth breath. Felix says, "We're gonna do it now." The stripper tries to pull away from his grip. "Come on, Felix. I said later. You're scaring me." He tightens it as she struggles. It's gonna get scarier if you don't give me what I want." Felix tightens his grip. "Get your fucking hands off me." Felix tries to rip off her robe and she fights him off. He holds her by the neck and pushes her into the corner. "Let me go, Felix. I told you after, you fucking asshole. Now you ain't getting shit." Felix pins her to the wall and tries to kiss her. She pushes him off and takes a swing at him but misses.

"You tried to hit me, you bitch." Felix punches her in the face and her head hits the steam pipe. She tries to scream but Felix covers her mouth. Her eyes are wide open and she's terrified. She pushes him off her again. She says "I'm telling Antonio."

Felix lunges at her and grabs her neck with both hands. Her eyes bulge as his grip tightens. She slowly sinks to the floor. Felix says "You ain't telling Antonio shit." Felix continues to hold her by the throat and she goes limp. Felix catches himself and realizes she may be dead. He panics and calls her name "Evelyn! Evelyn, wake up! Come on, wake up. Don't fuck around." Felix shakes her and slaps her face trying to wake her but she's not moving. He begins to talk to himself: "Felix, what the fuck did you do? You killed her, you stupid fuck! Antonio's gonna kill me. Shit! what the fuck do I do?" And he begins to sob." He pulls himself together and calls Antonio.

---

Anna has already left for her class. Antonio sits on the couch, watching the ballgame. He promised Anna he wouldn't drink but he's drinking anyway.

He's out of his element. Being home at night is something he's not used to. He's bored and he's looking for something to do. He promised Anna he would be home and he's trying his best to keep it. He notices the book about Stained Glass and he picks it up and leafs through the pages. Toward the end of the book he sees a picture. It's a photo of Tom's family, the same portrait hanging in Tom's house. Antonio is getting angry and begins to connect imaginary dots. They're both home all day, she lied about the book, the medals, the whispering all feed his jealousy. He shoves the picture into his pocket and puts the book back where he found it. He paces, thinking what to do. His cell phone rings but he's not in the mood to talk to anyone. Caller ID tells him it's Felix.

He picks up and he's angry. "What Felix?"

Felix says "Antonio, Antonio I fucked up, man. You gotta come."

"What happened Felix, you get busted again?"

"No Antonio. This is bad. Real bad."

"Where are you?"

"I'm at the club. You gotta come."

"I got my own shit I'm dealing with. This better not be some dumb shit."

"No, man. Antonio, you gotta come."

"Wait there, don't you go nowhere." Antonio grabs his coat and heads for the front door and it slams behind him.

Antonio walks in to Ball Breakers and he's greeted by the regulars. He looks around for Felix but doesn't see him. He walks over to his crew playing pool and he asks, "Yo, anybody see Felix." Some of the players say they haven't seen him. One player says "He's in the back." Antonio walks to the back room, and it's empty. He turns to the pool players and yells angrily "Which fucking room is he in?" One of the players says, "The ladies room—must be having his period." There's laughter as Antonio goes to the ladies room and knocks. No answer. He pounds the door with his fist. He yells, "Felix, open up." From inside Felix says, questioning, "Antonio, is that you?"

"Open the door." Felix has to move the stripper's body to open the door. Even then the door doesn't open all the way. The door opens wide enough for Antonio to squeeze through. He sees Felix against the sink, looking down.

"Felix, what the fuck did you do? Did you drop acid or . . . " Antonio stops in mid-sentence when he sees the stripper's legs. He slams the door and locks it. He stares at the stripper and looks at Felix. Antonio asks, "Is she dead?" Felix nods, still whimpering. "What the fuck did you do?"

"I don't know—we did a few rocks and she went nuts. Look, she scratched me on my face and my arms. I was trying to get her off me."

"So you're telling me she got high and tried to kill you. Was it my shit, Felix - and don't bullshit me."

"Yeah, the shit you gave me."

"No way, man. My stuff is clean. She never did that with me."

"I swear."

"No Felix, let me tell you what happened. You got high together and you decided you wanted some pussy. She told you no so you figured you'll just take it. She wasn't giving it up to a piece of shit like you."

Felix is crying now. "I swear she came after me. I didn't..."

Antonio doesn't give Felix a chance to finish the sentence. He grabs Felix around the neck with his right hand. Felix is shocked with how fast Antonio moved and grabbed his neck. He stares at Antonio with his eyes wide. He can't speak.

Antonio says, "It happened like I said, right? Tell me the truth or there's gonna be two dead people in this room." Felix nods in the affirmative. Antonio doesn't let go right away. He stares at Felix, holding onto his neck. Felix's eyes are bulging and his head is going from side to side. Antonio finally lets go. Felix wheezes and coughs, trying to catch his breath. Antonio paces in the tight space.

"What the fuck are we gonna do?"

Antonio is tapping his forehead with the heel of his hand.

Felix says, "Antonio."

"Felix, shut up."

"I'm sorry, Antonio."

"I'm gonna kill you, Felix, if you don't shut up." He says to himself, "Come on, Antonio. Think." He paces, looking at the stripper and Felix. He takes out his car keys and hands them to Felix. He says "Go get my car and back it up to the back room and open the trunk. Come back here and don't talk to anybody. You hear me?"

"Ok, you got a plan."

"Do what the fuck I say. Felix. Do it now." Felix leaves the room and Antonio is now alone in the bathroom. He looks down at the stripper's body. He's disgusted by the sight of her swollen face and bruises. He takes some paper towels and covers her face. Just then there's a knock on the door. Antonio listens and says, "Yeah." It was one of the strippers; her set just finished.

She says "Hey, pal. That's the ladies room and I gotta pee."

Antonio says, "It's out of order."

"Bullshit. Open up."

Antonio shouts back, "Get the fuck out of here." The stripper goes to the men's room as she mumbles to herself "fucking drug addicts."

Antonio listens by the door for Felix. The knock comes, startling Antonio. Antonio says, "Yeah."

"It's me, Antonio." Antonio opens the door and Felix comes in.

"The cars in the back by the door."

"Listen to me. Here's what we're gonna do. We're gonna stand her up, you on one side and me on the other. We take her to the back room. It'll look like she's drunk or stoned or something. When we get to the back, we put her on the table. I got garbage bags back there. Wait here. I'm gonna go unlock the door."

Antonio comes back to the bathroom. He says, "The door's unlocked." He takes the paper towels off her face, wets them and wipes off the dried blood.

Antonio says "Come on, grab one side. Let's get her on her feet." The men struggle with the dead weight. Antonio thought her body would be colder. Felix, the weaker of the two, is having a hard time. Her head is resting on Felix's shoulder and he begins to sob. "Man up, motherfucker Were you crying when you killed her? You can't go out there crying."

"I'm ok, I'm ok. Let's go."

The two men have control of the body. It looks like she's passed out as the men carry her to the back. Nobody pays any attention as the music keeps playing and the dancers keep dancing. This is a common occurrence in a place like this. The men open the door to the back room and go in. Antonio locks the door. They put the body on the table. Antonio says "Get the bags." Felix gets the garbage bags and hands the box to Antonio.

They begin wrapping the body in the bags.

Outside in the club, the bartender is looking for her since she's next on stage. He goes to the ladies room and knocks on the door. He shouts "Evelyn, you're on. Let's go." No answer from inside. He pounds on the door with his fist. "Evelyn! Open up. You're on." He opens the door and sees the bloody paper towels on the floor. He leaves the bathroom and knocks on the back room door.

"He shouts, "Evelyn, Evelyn!"

The body is partially wrapped on the table. The men stop and don't make a sound. Antonio whispers to Felix, "You got my keys?" Felix says, "Yeah."

The bartender says, "Come on, Evelyn. Are you getting high in there? Open up."

Antonio asks Felix, "Is the trunk open?"

Felix says, "Yeah." Antonio says "We're gonna pick her up and put her in the trunk. "Go ahead, Felix. Take her legs."

Antonio asks, "You ready?" The men lift the body and half carry and half drag her to the car.

They unceremoniously throw her into the trunk. The body lands with a thud. Antonio closes the trunk and gives Felix the keys.

He says, "Here, go park the car on the corner and wait for me. Don't come back into the club."

Felix drives away and Antonio closes the back door. He looks around the room to make sure it looks normal. He unlocks the front door and sits at the table drinking a beer. The bartender knocks again, calling Evelyn's name.

Antonio yells, "It's open."

The bartender walks in, sees Antonio and asks, "Why didn't you answer the door?"

Antonio says "I just got back."

The bartender says "Got back? I didn't see you leave."

Antonio says, "Yeah, Evelyn was fucked up. We put her in a cab. Me and Felix took her out the back."

The bartender, now agitated, says, "How come nobody told me she was leaving?"

Antonio replies angrily, "She was fucked up. We put her in a cab. What's the big deal?

"The big deal is she works for me. I gotta know this shit."

"Like I said, she was fucked up and we sent her home. Besides who are you to question what the fuck I do?"

"I'm her boss, that's who the fuck I am," the bartender says.

Antonio says, "You're the boss, so call up another bitch or get your fat ass up there and dance."

The bartender says, "What did you say to me?"

Antonio stands up with the bottle in his hand. He goes face to face with the bartender. He says "Fuck you, why don't you dance maricon?"

The bartender takes a swing at Antonio and connects. Antonio drops the bottle and stumbles into the main pool room. The bottle shatters on the floor getting everyone's attention. Antonio gets to his feet and grabs a pool cue. The pool players scatter and give the men room.

The bartender lunges at Antonio. Antonio swings the pool cue hitting the bartender on the side of the head. The bartender collapses and grabs the edge of the pool table to keep from falling to the floor. Antonio hits him again on the back of the head. The bartender tries to get up and Antonio hits him again snapping the cue in half. This time the bartender falls to the floor. One of the players says, "Stop, man. You're going to kill the dude," and he grabs the pool cue from his hand.

Antonio looks down at the bartender and comes to his senses. He remembers there's more important business at hand. Antonio runs from the club and to the car waiting on the corner. Felix is sitting in the passenger seat. Antonio jumps in and drives off.

Felix says, "Where were you, man?"

"We're fucked. I think I killed the bartender."

"What happened?"

"He was fucking with me, so I hit him with one of the pool sticks."

"Antonio, what if the cops stop us? We gotta…"

Antonio cuts him off, "Ain't nobody gonna rat me out. Don't worry."

Antonio drives to the waterfront area past junkyards and scrap metal salvage businesses. He stops in front of a gated auto junkyard. He jumps out of the car with a set of keys in his hand. He unlocks the gate and motions to Felix.

"Come on, help me with the gate. Help me get it open."

"Yo, where'd you get the keys?"

"I got 'em from some people I know," Antonio answers.

"Who? Those Mafia chumps that came to the club?"

"None of your business."

The men return to the car and drive into the yard. There are cars piled up in rows. Some are fairly new, some are rusted out hulks. Car parts are strewn everywhere. Antonio drives to the back of the junkyard and stops next to a big machine, a car crusher. Antonio gets out and opens the trunk.

Antonio turns to Felix and says, "Let's go, Felix."

Felix gets out of the car. Antonio is looking on the ground for something.

Felix asks, "What're you looking for?"

"See if you can find a pipe or something."

Felix comes up with a long piece of metal. He says, "Is this good?"

Antonio says "Yeah, help me pry open the trunk on that car." Antonio points to a car on the bottom of the pile next to the car crusher. The men struggle with the lock and, eventually, it pops open.

Antonio says, "Let's get her."

The men return to the car and lift the body out of the trunk. They carry the body to the rusted out hulk and put it in the trunk.

Antonio says, "I got some rope in the trunk. Go get it."

Antonio lowers the trunk lid on the junked car. Felix returns with the rope. The two men tie the trunk shut, "that's it Felix." Antonio looks around to make sure nothing was left behind.

Antonio says, "Let's get the fuck out of here."

The men get into Antonio's car and Felix has tears in his eyes. He's coming down from his high and the reality is hitting him. Antonio starts the car and drives to the front gate.

He tells Felix, "Go close the gates and don't forget to lock 'em. Here's the lock." Antonio hands the lock to Felix and rolls up the window. Antonio stares straight ahead. Felix closes the gates and gets back in the car.

As the men leave the waterfront, Antonio breaks the silence. They're gonna crush these cars. Then they melt 'em down. It takes seven thousand degrees to turn the metal to liquid. There'll be nothing left."

Felix is crying now and Antonio hears him and he says, "Cry all the fuck you want, but you owe me."

"I killed her. I ain't never killed nobody."

"Too late. She's dead."

"I'm sorry. I didn't mean it. I just wanted some pussy."

Antonio pulls the car over and stops. He sits quietly listening to Felix cry. Felix picks up his head and looks at Antonio, his eyes red. Felix says, "Why did you stop the car?"

Antonio is staring ahead and he says, "I helped you. Now you gotta help me."

Felix is whimpering and he says, "I'm sorry. I'm sorry. What do you want me to do?"

"You still driving that piece of shit car?"

"Yeah, why Antonio?"

"Cause I want you at my house tomorrow morning early."

"Your house. Why?"

"I want you to follow my wife."

"Your wife. Why?"

"Keep an eye on her. I wanna know everything she does."

There's silence in the car and Felix pulls himself together.

"I think she's fucking the guy upstairs."

"No way. You mean the old guy you told me about?"

"Let me tell you something about this guy, Felix. He's the real deal. He's a war hero and an ex-cop. He even does some martial arts shit. This guy's not soft."

"So what? Do I watch her?"

"That's what I said. Follow her."

"How long, Antonio? All day?

"Until I get home, Felix. You better be there at sunrise and make sure she doesn't see you."

"I'll be there. I won't fuck it up."

"There's the bus stop. Don't forget, Felix. Early. Now get out."

Felix gets out and Antonio drives off.

# CHAPTER 18

# ANNA'S FLIGHT
# (THE TRUTH HURTS)

Tom exits his apartment and walks to his car. It's a beautiful day with unlimited visibility so he decides to go flying. He's carrying a briefcase with his flight plans and charts. As he opens his car door, he notices Anna standing on her steps. He says, "Good morning Anna."

She walks toward his car and says, "Where are you off to so early?" - her hair wet from her shower.

Tom says, "I got a few things I need to take care of." Tom is standing by the open door, looking at Anna.

She's wondering what he's staring at and she says "What?"

Against his better judgment, he asks Anna to go with him. "Do you have plans for today?"

"No, not really."

"Would you like to come with me?"

"Where?"

"It's a surprise."

Anna hesitates, "I don't think it's a good idea. Antonio's working and I usually have his dinner ready when he gets home."

"What time do you have to be back?"

"By 2, I guess."

"Done. We'll be back before then."

"Why can't you tell me?"

"It won't be a surprise if I do."

"No, you go. I'm not dressed."

"Are you sure? I'll wait."

"You don't mind?"

"No, go ahead. I'll be here."

"What do I wear?"

"Something comfortable."

"I don't know, Tom. Can I trust you?"

"Of course you can trust me."

Anna asks, "Back by 2?"

"I promise. Back by 2."

"Ok, I'll go, but I have to change."

Tom is reading the flight plans when he looks up and sees Anna locking her front door. Anna is wearing a white flowing dress, her hair, still damp, is curly and thick. She opens the door and gets in.

"Did I take too long?"

"Nope."

Tom starts the car and they drive towards the airport. The car drives past Felix who's parked on the corner. He starts the car and follows.

Tom asks Anna, "You don't get air sick, do you?"

"No, are we going to Paris for dinner?"

"Can't. Gotta be back by two, remember?"

"Are you kidnapping me, Tom?"

"Yep, you guessed it."

"And the plane is your hideout."

Tom laughs and he makes a left turn onto the highway. Tom says, "We're almost there."

Anna is looking out the window and notices they're on the airport access road.

"Are you serious? We're going to the airport."

"You'll see." He follows the signs to Hangar G, which is Scottie's shop. Tom reaches the hangar and is pleased to see his plane is at the front of the runway.

Felix stops across the road and watches from inside his car. Tom exits the car and opens the passenger side door and helps Anna out. The mechanics stop to look at Anna as they walk into the hangar. Tom says to Scottie, "Hey, Scottie. How's it going?"

"Great, Tom. And who's this lovely lady?"

"This is Anna. Anna meet Scottie."

Scottie takes Anna's hand and kisses it. Tom says, "Watch out for Scottie. He's a ladies' man."

"Used to be." "These days my love is these babies you see in her," and he gestures to the planes in the hangar. So are you all set?"

Tom says, "Yeah, we're good."

Tom hands Scottie his flight plan. Scottie quickly looks at it. He says, "I'll get your paperwork. Be right back."

He leaves and goes to his office. Anna asks, "Tom, are we flying somewhere? Like a tour or something?"

Anna looks at the planes and says, "These planes are beautiful." She points to Tom's plane and says, "I love the red and white one."

"Well, this is your lucky day."

"Are we going in that one?"

"Yeah, that's the one."

Ann walks around the plane admiring it. Scottie returns and hands Tom some papers. He folds them and puts them in his jacket pocket.

"Thanks, Scottie."

"Happy flying. See ya when you get back."

Tom turns to Anna, "Are you ready?"

"I think so," Anna answers.

Tom takes Anna by the arm and walks her to the plane.

"Wait, isn't Scottie coming?"

"Nah, three's a crowd."

"But who's gonna fly the plane?"

"You're looking at him."

Anna says, surprised, "You?"

"Are you surprised?"

"How come you never told me?"

"Are you nervous?"

"A little. I've never been in a plane that small before."

Tom helps Anna into the plane and climbs in himself. They buckle their safety harnesses. Anna has a little trouble and Tom helps her buckle up.

Felix drives his car to the side of the hangar so he can see Tom's car. He settles in to wait until they get back.

The plane starts up and purrs as it taxies to the head of the runway. Tom is checking the gauges on the control panel and running a pre-flight check. Tom speaks into his mic on the headset. "Suffolk Airport Tower, this is Delta Charlie 4732. I'm ready for take off."

The voice on the other end says, "Good morning, Tom. Good flying day, ain't it? Proceed to #3 and climb to 8,000 feet. Baltimore ATC will pick you up. Over."

Tom says, "Copy. Going to 8,000. DC4732 Out." He pulls back on the throttle and the plane rolls down the runway picking up speed as it goes. The plane gets airborne and Anna holds her stomach as the plane climbs.

Tom says, "That was the toughest part."

Anna looks at Tom nervously and holds onto the arms of her seat.

"When we level off, it'll be a lot smoother. You sure you're ok?

Anna is still holding onto her seat. "I'm a little scared, but it's fun."

Anna is looking out the side window and she asks, "How high are we now?"

Tom says, "3,000 feet on the way to 8,000. That's the Long Island Sound down there."

Anna says, "It's beautiful."

The radio squawks, "Good morning DC4732. This is Baltimore ATC. We got you. Climb to 8,000 feet and hold. Do you copy?"

Tom says, "Good morning. This is DC4732. I copy. Over."

Anna is more relaxed and she asks, "How long have you been flying?"

Tom answers, "Since I left the military - about fifteen years. Do you like my plane?

"I love it. How old is it?"

"She was built in 1959. It's a Cessna 170. I found her in a boneyard."

"A boneyard?"

"It's a scrapyard. The owner was selling her. She belonged to his father."

"Was it in bad shape?"

"No, not that bad. I made him an offer and he was happy to get rid of her. You should have seen Scottie's face when I got it back to his hangar. He and I restored it. He's quite a mechanic."

"Is Scottie a pilot too?"

"Yeah, he's a great pilot. He helped me when I was learning how to fly.

"Wow, how long did it take you guys to fix it up?

"Two years and a little more than $27,000."

"She's beautiful. What's her name?"

Tom is confused and asks, "Her name?"

"Tom, she's gotta have a name."

"She does. Delta Charlie 4732." Tom says.

"No, a regular name. People name their boats, why not your plane?"

Tom smiles and shakes his head.

"Why are you smiling; you think I'm crazy."

Tom gestures out the window, "No, you're not crazy. Look out the window. Paris is 3,000 miles away.

Anna is looking out the window and she says, "The ocean is so vast, so scary."

"I was thinking about having lunch in Mystic, Connecticut."

"How far is that?"

"We could be there in an hour."

"If we go, we'll never get back by two, will we?"

"Is it really that important?"

"It is to Antonio."

"What about you?"

"Me? Antonio is my husband and there's things he expects from me."

"Like?"

"Like dinner, Tom. It's the least I can do. He works all day." Anna says. "Can we talk about something else?"

"We can, but I think he expects more than dinner from you."

"Tom, drop it, please."

"I just want you to be honest with yourself Anna."

"About what?"

"About your feelings for Antonio."

"My feelings for Antonio are none of your business."

Tom looks out the side window.

Anna says, "Why did you ask me to come today?"

Tom looks at Anna and says, "I thought you might need a change."

"From what? My boring life?"

"I didn't say that. You're right. It's none of my business."

The radio squawks, "This is Baltimore ATC, come in DC4732."

Tom responds, "Baltimore ATC, this is DC 4732. I'm at 8,000 feet."

"Hold at 8,000 DC 4732. Do you copy?"

"Copy Baltimore ATC, will hold at 8,000."

"Happy flying DC4732."

Anna is looking out the window.

Tom says, "We're gonna see Montauk pretty soon."

Anna is still looking out the window. She says, "Tom, you're a policeman. What do you know about my husband?"

"Nothing Anna. I retired before he got here."

"Did you ever ask your friends about him?"

"I don't have to. I already know."

"Know what, Tom?"

"I know you're in an abusive relationship."

"Don't talk to me that way, Tom."

"I know the signs, Anna. Like you said, I'm a policeman."

"You don't know anything about me and Antonio."

"I know you're afraid of him. When he's near you, you're tense and scared."

Anna turns away and looks out the window again. She is tearing up, but she doesn't want Tom to know. The cabin is silent for a while.

Anna asked, "When you were a policeman, did you ever kill anybody?"

Tom doesn't answer.

"I'm sorry Tom. You don't have to answer."

Tom finally says, "Yes."

Anna turns and looks at Tom, looks back outside the front window. She says, "I feel like I can stay up here forever. It's beautiful, quiet and peaceful, but at the same time, it's dangerous, just like you Tom. Please take me back."

"If that's what you want."

"Sorry if I ruined your day, Tom."

Scottie and a mechanic are in the hangar and Scottie hears Tom's plane coming in. He looks at his watch and says, "That ain't right. He's back too soon."

Scottie walks fast to the front of the hangar as Tom's plan taxies in. Scottie says, "You're back early. Is everything ok?"

Tom says, "Yeah, with the plane."

"Do me a favor, would you help Anna down?"

Scottie walks around to the passenger side as Anna struggles with her seat belt.

"Scottie, could you please help me with this?"

Scottie points to the red button in the middle of the belt and tells Anna "Just give it some slack and push the red button."

"Thank you, Scottie." Anna says.

"You're welcome Anna. Tom went to get the car."

"I'm afraid he's not very happy with me right now. I kinda messed up his plans."

Scottie says, "He'll be ok in a little while. He won't be upset for long."

Tom's car drives up and stops by Scottie and Anna. Scottie opens the door and Anna gets in the car. Tom's window goes down and he says, "Scottie, take care. Thanks."

Scottie says to Anna, "Don't forget what I told you."

She extends her hand and Scottie kisses it. "It was nice to meet you."

Scottie says, "See ya."

Tom and Anna are sitting silently. Anna is looking out the side window.

Tom says, "I need to go to the house. I have more stuff to bring to the apartment."

Anna says, "Can you drop me off at the market? I'll walk from there."

Tom's car drives into the parking lot of the market. Anna reaches into the back for her bag. She retrieves it, looks at Tom and says, "Tom, it's my fault the day turned out this way."

"I never should've brought it up."

Anna pauses and says, "You were right about Antonio."

"What?"

"You were right about him."

Tom is looking at Anna and he says, "A couple of days ago, you told me I don't have to be alone. Do you remember?"

Anna nods and says, "Yes. We were in your apartment."

"Well, you don't have to accept the abuse."

Anna looks at Tom. She opens the door and exits the car. She walks towards the market, turns and waves goodbye to Tom. Tom turns out of the parking lot. Felix is tailing him as he drives towards his house on Oak Street.

Tom arrives at his house and goes up the stairs and enters, the door closing behind him. Felix parks across the street and watches. Tom grabs a beer from the fridge and sits on the couch. He looks around the room and admires the remaining stained glass panels still hanging in the windows and thinks about Rebecca. He wonders if taking the apartment in Anna's house was a bad idea.

# CHAPTER 19

# FELIX BEARS WITNESS

A cab stops in front of Tom's house and Anna gets out. Felix is half asleep having smoked half a joint, which is typical for Felix. Seeing Anna going up the steps snaps him out of his stupor. He says to himself, "What the fuck?"

Anna gets to the door and rings the bell. Tom opens it and is surprised to see Anna standing there. She walks in and says, "Tom, I need to talk to you."

"Come in, Anna. Are you ok?"

"No, Tom." Anna stands in front of Tom and Tom tries to go around her to the living room. She blocks his path and she says, "Tom, look at me and tell me what you're feeling right now."

"Anna, this is no good. You're married."

Anna says, "Please tell me."

Tom tries to go around her again, but she follows him, takes his arm and turns him so they're face to face. Tom looks into Anna's eyes for a few seconds, then takes her into his arms and kisses her passionately.

Felix watches from his car as Anna returns his kiss and puts her arms around his shoulders, their silhouettes visible through the stained glass in the window. He thinks to himself, "Antonio's gonna kill that dude."

Tom picks her up and carries her to the couch. They fall to the couch and continue kissing as they begin to undress each other. The sunlight coming through the stained glass casts colors on their semi-naked bodies.

Felix has his head back. He's still stoned and he looks at his watch. It's 1:15

---

Tom and Anna are lying in bed. Anna says, "Be careful Tom. Antonio carries a gun."

"I figured as much. I can take care of myself. Do you know if he ever used it?"

"We don't talk about it. I never wanted to ask how your wife died. I felt I didn't have the right."

"Do you want to know?"

"Not now, Tom. Not if it upsets you."

"She died in surgery—a routine operation."

"My God, Tom. I'm so sorry."

Tom continues, "I was at work when Rebecca called me. She told me she was having bad stomach pain. I drove to the house and my neighbor told me she was taken by ambulance to Hampton General. When I got there, a nurse told me that she was in surgery.

Her appendix almost burst, but they caught it in time and she would be out of surgery in a few hours. I felt relieved, but two hours became three and then four. I was trying to find someone who could explain why it was taking so long. When a nurse came out, I feared the worst. The look on her face said it all. She told me that Rebecca didn't survive the surgery. A lot of emotion went through me, shock, anger, and sorrow.

"I asked her why didn't the doctor come out to speak to me. I demanded to see him. She told me he was unavailable. My darling Rebecca was dead and he couldn't come out to tell me how or why. In a fit of anger, I went to the operating room with the nurse attempting to calm me down. When I burst into the room, I saw Rebecca's body under a blood-soaked sheet. Again, I demanded to see the doctor. I picked up a tray of instruments and threw them across the room.

I pulled back the sheet and lying there was Rebecca, her eyes closed. The color had left her face. I fell to my knees. I felt hands grab me by the arms and shoulders and drag me out of the room. I was taken to a small chapel. A deep voice told me if I didn't calm down, they would have to call the police. As a cop, I understood they were just doing their job. Damn rent-a-cops stayed with me until a doctor came in. He told me he was the chief of staff. I asked him what happened to Rebecca. He told me while they were getting a team together, her appendix burst and caused severe bleeding. They couldn't get it under control. He said they tried everything but the infection and bleeding was too much. He told me he was sorry. About a month later, I got a call from a nurse who was in the operating room. That night, the resident on duty was not experienced to handle a complicated surgery. Dr. Weeks, chief of surgery, was called to come in. When he arrived, he was obviously intoxicated, and in our opinion, should not have been in the O.R. Dr. Ramos, the resident, said he would do the surgery if Dr. Weeks would talk him through it. We felt this was the best way to proceed.

At least the instruments would be in steady hands. Dr. Weeks refused and he told Dr. Ramos that he was only a resident and he should watch and learn. We objected and Dr. Weeks silenced us. With time running out, we had to give in. You see, Dr. Weeks threatened us with disciplinary action if we protested. Dr. Ramos tried his best to assist, but from the moment the surgery began, we realized hope for Rebecca was fading. She was bleeding and we couldn't stop it. As her vital signs were fading, Dr. Weeks stormed out of the O.R. Rebecca died a short time later. Drunk and unsteady, Dr. Weeks cut into the appendix and caused bacteria to spread. He didn't clamp the veins properly and the bleeding was uncontrollable. I haven't had a good night's sleep since it happened. I had to tell you."

I asked her if she would testify against Dr Weeks. She told me if she did she would never work in nursing again. There's a code of silence that runs through the medical profession. She told me she wanted to be a nurse since she was a little girl. She loved being a nurse. I didn't want to do anything to destroy her future. I felt bad for her. She was innocent in this."

"What did you do?"

"It took me a few months of searching for him. I called hospitals but nobody knew him. He had a pile of malpractice suits and a drug rap. I tracked him down and finally I found him in Costa Rica."

"What happened when you found him?"

Tom is staring at the ceiling and he says "I killed him."

---

Felix has his seat back, his eyes half closed and he looks at his watch. Anna has been in Tom's house for three hours. He's looking forward to telling Antonio what he saw. Felix is a crack addicted loser who lives vicariously through Antonio. It gives him pleasure to see turmoil in other people's lives.

A taxi stops in front of Tom's house. Anna exits the house in a hurry, goes down the steps and into the taxi. The taxi leaves and drives past Felix. Felix starts the car and follows the taxi. It stops in front of Anna's house and she goes in. Felix drives off excited about telling Antonio what he saw. Antonio is playing pool with the regulars. His cell phone rings and he answers "Yeah, Felix. What's up."

"Yo, it's like you said, man. Your wife is playing you."

"Don't fuck with me Felix. You better be sure."

Felix can hardly contain himself "Yeah, I'm sure. They went into a house on Oak Street. I could see them through the window."

Antonio's anger is now at its peak "That motherfucker! Where are you now?"

"I'm outside your house. Your wife is home. I'll meet you at the dude's house. We'll fuck him up."

"You're a stupid man, Felix. I got something else planned for the war hero. Meet me at the junkyard. Remember—the one where we dumped that girl you killed?"

"Come on, man. Don't say it like that. It was an accident."

"Be there in an hour."

Tom leaves his house on Oak Street and drives to his apartment. He goes into the bedroom, reaches under the bed and pulls out a metal box. He opens the box and inside are three guns and two boxes of ammo. Tom picks up a small gun in a holster with velcro fasteners. He takes the gun out of the holster to see if it's loaded and attaches the holster to his ankle. He takes a bottle of beer out of the fridge, goes outside and sits on the steps to his apartment.

Felix is sitting in Antonio's car, telling Antonio what happened that day. Antonio is angry. "So how long were they in the house?"

"Three hours."

"Just what I thought—the war hero is messing with my wife."

"I know what his plane looks like. Let's go burn that shit."

"Nah, Felix I don't give a shit about his plane. It's him."

"So whatcha gonna do, Antonio?"

Antonio stares straight ahead as he speaks. "We're gonna kill the war hero."

"We, Antonio? I can't kill nobody."

"Oh no, you already did, remember."

Antonio turns to Felix with a cold stare and he points to the junkyard "She's over there in one of the cars."

"I ain't gonna do it, Antonio."

"Yes, you are. We're gonna do him together. You're gonna help me."

"I ain't killing nobody. I'll tell the cops you wanna kill the guy." Antonio looks straight ahead. A sick smile on his face. He reaches into the side pocket of his jacket. Felix jumps not sure what to expect from him. Antonio takes out a video cassette from a camcorder and shows it to Felix. Antonio says, "Relax, you little pussy. Do you know what this is?"

"Yeah, some kind of film."

"You wanna guess what's in this film?"

"What?"

"You and the stripper, Felix. I put a camera in the ceiling so I could watch those bitches. You'd be surprised what they do in there."

"Yeah but you're in there, too."

"It's funny, but that part of the tape got erased. You still wanna go to the cops?"

Felix's voice is cracking and he says, "Why are you doing this to me, man? I don't want to kill anybody."

"You're gonna help me, Felix, and that's it. I gotta big score coming soon. You and me are gonna kill the war hero. I get paid and then I'm out."

"What about me, man?"

"What about you? You keep playing pool and hanging out with those pendejos. Now get out. I'll let you know when."

Felix exits the car and walks to the bus stop on the corner. The driver's side window goes down, and Antonio looks at the film cassette in his hand with a smile on his face. "What a stupid fuck! Who uses camcorders anymore?" He throws the cassette out the window and drives off.

# CINNAMON CALLING

DiNapoli is in the social club playing cards. He's sitting at a table with his crew, Dom, Primo, and two local button men. The old school phone on the wall rings. Richie says "Hey, Dom. Get the phone."

"Hey Richie, why is it always me who gets the phone?"

"Come on. Get the fucking phone. Don't be a dick." Dom slams his cards down on the table and walks to pick up the phone. Richie picks up Dom's cards and shows them to the other players.

"Don't worry, Dom. I won't let them see your cards." The men snicker as Dom picks up the phone and answers, "Yeah?"

A female voice asks, "Is this DiNapoli Carting."

"Ahh yeah, DiNapoli Carting. That's right."

"Is Mr. DiNapoli there?"

Dom covers the phone and shouts to Richie, "Hey, Richie. You here?"

Richie responds, "Depends on who it is."

"Some broad."

"Don't say broad! Do you live in a fucking cave? I'll be right there." Richie walks to the phone, "This is Richie, who's this?"

"Mr. DiNapoli, was that your secretary? Does she have a cold?"

Richie laughs. "That's not my secretary, that's a friend of mine. He works for me, who are you?"

"I'm someone who's holding your card."

"A lot of people hold my card. Let me guess, auburn hair, body to die for, too good for that place you dance in."

"You're getting warm."

"You remind me of a spice."

"Very good, Mr. DiNapoli."

"You working tonight, Cinnamon?"

"Yeah, till midnight."

"You like champagne?"

"Champagne? Who doesn't?"

"I know a place that's got fountains of it. See you at midnight."

"Sure of ourselves, aren't we?"

"Just say no and I'll go away."

"See you at midnight."

It's a little after midnight and Cinnamon is leaving the club. She sees a black limousine and walks toward it. The back window goes down as Primo goes around the back of the car to open the door for her. From inside the car Richie says, "Come in, Cinnamon. I don't bite. Don't be afraid."

Cinnamon responds, "Maybe you should be afraid of me," as she steps in and sits next to DiNapoli.

DiNapoli looks at Cinnamon and asks, "Were you dancing all night?"

"Yeah, about six hours."

"Well, if you look this good after work, I'd like to see you after a good night's sleep."

"That's original. I never heard that before."

"It's not a line—you're gorgeous!"

"So, Mr. DiNapoli, where's this place with fountains of champagne?"

"Please, call me Richie. Primo, to The Empire Club."

"The Empire Club, that's posh."

"You've been there?"

"No, over my budget I'm afraid."

"That's 'cause you're dancing in a dump out on the island. What're you making now, two-fifty a night? A dancer with your looks and that killer body should be pulling down five, six hundred a night. I got some people in Manhattan who run some high-end clubs I can . . ."

Cinnamon cuts him off. "Thanks, Richie, we can talk about it some other time."

Richie asks, "What's your name."

"Cinnamon."

"No, I mean your real name. Isn't Cinnamon your stripper, I'm sorry, dancing name?"

"No, it's my name and don't apologize. I know what I do to pay the bills."

"So how did you get into it?"

"It's a long story. I needed money for rent, food, credit cards. You know. Things didn't go according to plan. I thought I'd be making some big money."

"You can, but not there."

She glances out the window and sees the New York Skyline from the Queensboro Bridge and says, "Beautiful, isn't it?"

"Yeah, but it hides a lot of shit."

"What do you really know about me—who I am, what I do? You gave me your card. It says you're in the carting business."

"Come on. You know what I'm asking."

"Just what I read and hear."

"Does it bother you what you hear about me."

"We're in a limo together and we seem to be getting along. I don't have a problem with it." They both chuckle.

Cinnamon asks, "How'd you get into it?"

"I'm taking the fifth. It's too complicated. Primo, didn't I tell you to take the tunnel, it's faster."

"Yeah boss, but I just saved you about twenty bucks."

"But it's costing 25 bucks in gas."

Cinnamon asks, "Does he work for you?"

"Yeah, I got a big payroll to look after." Richie lowers his voice. "He's not the brightest bulb, but he's so loyal, it's scary. To me, loyalty is very important.

Cinnamon asks, "What does he do, is he like a bodyguard or something?"

"You don't want to know what he does, let's leave it at that. Besides, we're almost there."

"Ok, Richie."

"You hungry?"

"Yeah, starved."

"This place has the best filet mignon in the city. You're in for a treat. The owner is a friend of mine. Here we are."

They leave the car and enter the restaurant. Hours later they arrive at Richie's house on Long Island by the shore. It's four a.m. Primo opens the door and helps Richie out of the car. Richie has had a lot to drink and is feeling the effects. Primo extends his hand to Cinnamon and she exits the car much soberer than Richie.

Richie asks, "Hey Primo, how many times have you been to the Brooklyn Aquarium?"

"What, boss?"

"How many times have you been there, you know, the Aquarium?"

"I don't know, boss. Maybe ten or twelve times, I guess."

"Do you like fish that much, Primo?"

Cinnamon is a little embarrassed for Primo and she tries to intercede. "I like the Aquarium, too, Richie."

"That's nice, but I'm talking to Primo."

"Tell you what Primo. Take tomorrow off. Go see some whales or sharks or whatever the fuck. It's Wednesday and I got a meeting at the club."

"You sure, boss?"

"Yeah, I'm sure. Take the day off. Why do you go there anyway, Primo?"

"Cause it relaxes me from all this bullshit."

"So Primo, you're saying what we do is bullshit—is that what you think?"

"I'm not talking about that. I mean the world, you know, war and all that shit."

Richie asks Cinnamon, "You like fish, too. Do they relax you, babe, or is it bullshit?"

Cinnamon says, "They're fun to watch, and yeah, they relax me. Now can we go inside, please? I'm fucking exhausted." Richie says, "I decide when we go inside."

He turns to Primo and says, "What the fuck are you doing here?"

"We were talking about fish. Remember, boss?"

Richie says "We're done talking. So go, get the fuck out of here and be careful driving. You're drunk."

Primo walks to the limo driver's side and turns to Richie and says, "I'm not drunk, boss. Am I off tomorrow?"

"Sure Primo, take off, do whatever the fuck you want."

"Thanks, boss."

"Hey, Primo, say hello to Flipper."

Richie turns to Cinnamon and says, "We love Flipper. Don't we, babe?"

Cinnamon replies, "Richie, can we go inside now? I'm freezing out here."

"Ok, babe, let's go. Primo's gonna go visit Orca tomorrow. I hope a shark bites him on the ass." Richie laughs as he staggers into the house, being helped by Cinnamon.

# CHAPTER 21

# PRIMO DELICATO

Primo is enjoying his day off. He made a fine marinara sauce with meatballs and sliced the garlic hair thin so it would dissolve in the sauce. He sautéed some fresh broccoli rabe and got a loaf of just-baked Italian bread. He pours himself a glass of MontePulciano 2012 and sets the table for one, with cloth napkins and silverware. His apartment is neat but hasn't been updated since his mother died ten years ago. He's dressed for dinner with a black suit, white shirt, and black tie, and his gun is always with him in a shoulder holster. Family pictures and pictures of patron saints are hung around the living room. In a display case is his mother's collection of thimbles from all over the world, a collection she was very proud of and she would show them to everyone who came to the house. Opera music plays in the background while Primo mimics the conductor with a wooden spoon, waving the spoon all around like a conductor's baton. He even sings along with the music, entirely off-key.

The pasta is ready, al dente of course, and he drains it and lets it drip. He puts the right amount of sauce on top and sprinkles freshly grated cheese on the sauce. He sits at the table, tucks a napkin into his collar and turns on the television. He surfs the channels looking for a movie but he stops at the six 'o'clock news. They're breaking a story about an organized crime murder from two years ago. They're reporting the authorities have new evidence regarding the murder of an organized crime associate, and the associate's name was Salvator 'Sallie Boy' Nardo. He was a member of the Scarpello crime family. Authorities believe the DiNapoli crime family ordered the hit on 'Sallie Boy' through their many associates. As of now, investigators are tight-lipped about the identity of the killer or killers. Nardo was found face down in an alleyway, with his neck broken and shot twice in the head. Investigators see a connection between this murder and two others with the same MO.

"We'll have more information …" Primo changes the channel, and he is staring at the TV as if in a trance. He shakes his head from side to side hoping to wake himself from a nightmare, breathing heavily, he takes a sip of wine to calm himself. He begins to sweat and he takes a fork full of pasta and shoves it into his mouth. His anxiety is growing and he pushes the plate of pasta away, while on the stove his broccoli rabe is beginning to burn. He gets up and turns off the burner and sits back down. He takes another sip of wine and begins to mumble to himself. "It can't be. I was careful. There's no way they know. It's bullshit. Yeah, it's just bullshit." He has more wine and he's beginning to calm down.

He's channel surfing one reality show after another, and finally, he finds something that interests him. It's a documentary about sharks. Primo stops and is fixated on the image of sharks killing and devouring a small whale. Blood and flesh litter the water as the sharks tear apart the whale. The whale thrashes in the water as the sharks continue to prey on the whale, as the blood in the water increases the frenzy. Primo is aroused by the power of the sharks and the blood as they rip flesh from the whale, and he takes another sip of wine. His right-hand goes to his zipper, he opens his pants and masturbates. Watching the feeding frenzy brings him to the point of no return and he climaxes. The table shakes and the plates rattle as he holds on the table in ecstasy. It's over, his head goes back, his eyes close and he begins to snore.

# CHAPTER 22

# MOMMY ISSUES

Cinnamon calls Sergeant McMahon. "Hello, Cinnamon. How's it going? Talk to me."

Cinnamon responds. "Our boy Sanchez had some visitors a few nights ago."

"Who?"

"Richie DiNapoli and a few of his paisans. They went into that back room that Sanchez hangs out in. The bartender told me Sanchez is the only one with a key. He uses it as some bullshit office. One of the guys was carrying a briefcase and a big dude was watching the door."

"Let me see. The guy with the briefcase was . . . "

Cinnamon cuts her off. "Dom, and the other guy was Primo. From my vantage point, I saw the whole thing."

"Vantage point, what do you mean?"

"I'm on stage, Sarge. Remember, I'm a stripper."

"What about Sanchez, anything else on him?"

"No, except he's a real piece of work. He tried to talk me into that back room of his."

"No shit! What did he say?"

"He promised me drugs and all the shit he can do with his tongue……"

McMahon cuts her off—"That's enough of that."

"I told him if he didn't leave me alone my boyfriend was gonna break his legs."

"Shit, Cinnamon. Who's your boyfriend?"

"Richie DiNapoli."

There was silence on the other end of the phone. "Are you serious? How the fuck did that happen?"

"It's called irony, Sarge. I was dancing the night DiNapoli and Sanchez had their meeting. Richie came out and watched me dance. He gave me his card and here we are."

McMahon is angry and it shows in her voice. "Here we are, that's it? I'm hearing about this now. Are you sleeping with him, agent?"

"Did you just call me 'agent'? Goddamn, you must really be pissed off! Look Sarge, I'm sleeping with him, but it's not what you think."

"Then what is it? Why're you sleeping with him? Do you want me to pull you from this case?"

"No, I don't. Please hear me out. Richie's got issues, Sarge."

"Issues, what do you mean?"

"I think it's mommy issues. He doesn't touch me—he just wants to cuddle, and he calls for his mommy in his sleep."

"Are you kidding? Shit, how weird! We got a tough guy with mommy issues. You can't make this shit up."

"There's more. He talks in his sleep and keeps me awake."

"What does he say?"

"He babbles most of the time. But there's something he does every night in his sleep. He repeats the number 82 over and over."

"82? What do you think it means?"

"I don't know Sarge, but I'll try to find out."

"Be careful Cinnamon. Mommy issues or not, DiNapoli is a dangerous man."

# CHAPTER 23

# THE SHEFFIELD DINER

Antonio is in the club shooting pool with Felix when his phone rings.

"Who's this."

The voice on the other end says "You forgot me already—my feelings are hurt. I think we should continue our talk from the other night."

"No way, Rodriguez. We're done. Stay the fuck away from me."

Rodriguez ignores him and asks, "You know the Sheffield Diner? Be there tonight at ten."

"For what?"

"See you there," Rodriguez replies forcefully.

The diner is about 12 miles out of town on Rt. 25. It's a hole in the wall that always seems to survive the health inspector. Rodriguez gets there early and takes a seat overlooking the parking lot. A little after ten Sanchez arrives and sits across from Rodriguez.

"So I'm here. Now what?"

Rodriguez asks, "How are things at Ball Breakers?"

"You dragged me out here for that shit?"

"You banging strippers, Antonio?"

"You know I'm married, Rodriguez. So don't try that shit on me."

The waitress shows up and asks, "You boys want anything?"

Rodriguez says, "Sure. A cup of coffee and a toasted bagel—well done."

Rodriguez asks Sanchez, "You want anything?"

"You crazy—look at this place—it's filthy!"

The waitress glares at Sanchez, as Rodriguez says, "Don't worry, darling. He's in a bad mood, and you're a great waitress."

"Fuck you. Rodriguez! Eat your bagel by yourself. I'm out!"

He reaches into the pocket of his jacket and takes out a baggie full of white powder and puts it on the table and asks, "What does that look like to you?"

Sanchez says, "Come on, man. Put that away."

The couple at the table next to them look over at the men. Rodriguez again asks "What is this stuff?" Just then the waitress brings the bagel and coffee for Rodriguez. She places the food on the table, notices the baggie with the powder, shakes her head and walks away.

Rodriguez nonchalantly takes a teaspoon of white powder, waves it around and asks, "You want some?"

Sanchez looks around and says, "You crazy, man."

Rodriguez puts the white powder in his coffee. He stirs the coffee looking at Rodriguez. "This time it's sugar. Next time, who knows? Ten or fifteen of these baggies filled with something other than sugar found in the trunk of your car would cause a lot of trouble for you."

"You gonna plant shit on me? That's illegal, and you gotta prove it's mine. This ain't nothing but a shakedown! You can't keep me here, I'm out."

Rodriguez sits sipping his coffee unfazed by what Sanchez said. He looks up at Sanchez and leans back in the booth. "I heard you got a private room in the back. What goes on there, Sanchez?"

"How the fuck should I know. Maybe lap dances?"

"You should know Sanchez, you're the only one with a key."

"I'm out." Sanchez storms out of the coffee shop. The waitress brings Rodriguez the check and he says, "Told you he was in a bad mood."

# CHAPTER 24
## JORGE DELACRUZ

Jorge Delacruz is sitting at a long table with his associates. Delacruz is the head of the most powerful drug cartel in Colombia. He's short in stature, pudgy with pox marks on his face. He's in his mid-50s and has gray hair that he dyes an awful shade of brown. People who know him say he's a humble, sophisticated and educated man, but people who have crossed him are dead. He's on Interpol's 'most wanted' list, but massive payoffs to police and politicians insulate him.

The men are gathered at a beautiful hacienda in Medellin, Colombia. Tapestries, priceless artwork and expensive rugs from around the world adorn the walls and marble floors. Ornate fountains and pools are located throughout the hacienda, and frolicking in these pools are beautiful women. Delacruz and his associates are having lunch. There are plates of caviar, lobsters, fine wines and champagne.

A manservant comes to clear the table while Delacruz sits back and speaks.

"Gentlemen, did you enjoy your lunch?" The men at the table nod in agreement. "Yes, gentlemen, I know—lobster, caviar, the finest wines—who can deny it? Look at me, do I look like a movie star?"

The men look at each other, not understanding the question.

"Come on, don't be afraid. Be honest."

One of the men at the table named Miguel says, "No, Padrone, but...."

Delacruz cuts him off. "An honest man, but allow me to answer. I'm a rather unattractive man but look at how I live, the Palacio, the art, the food, but best of all the women. Look at them laughing and enjoying themselves. Anytime I want I could select one or all if I choose, go to my bedroom and we'd make love until the sun comes up. On the other hand, if I choose to kill one and bury her in the jungle I could do that too."

The men are uneasy, and they shift in their seats and glance at each other. Delacruz says "I see I made you uneasy, tranquillo, gentlemen. Why would I hurt such beautiful creatures?"

At that point, the manservant brings cigars to Delacruz. He places the cigars on the right side of the table, and Delacruz says to his manservant, "Thank you. Gentlemen, cigars! They're not from Cuba—fuck Cuba. These are specially made for me. Let's enjoy them." Delacruz passes around the cigars. The manservant lights Delacruz's cigar first then proceeds around the table, and Delacruz says to his manservant, "Thank you. You can go home to your family now, I won't need you the rest of the day."

"Are you sure, Padrone? It's still early."

"Yes, you may go." The manservant thanks him and leaves. Delacruz speaks to the others. "My manservant is the wealthiest servant in Colombia. He has a beautiful hacienda not far from here, a beautiful wife, drives a nice car, anything he wants. Do you know why, gentlemen?" The men at the table glance at each other. "Loyalty. I buy it with money. Some of you at this table may be wondering why Tomas is not here. It'll tell you why. He betrayed me and he stole some of my merchandise. It seems he was offered a better deal across the river with that pendejo, El Moreno." He looks around the table at the men seated there. He takes a drag from his cigar and points to the men. "Gentlemen, if any of you are looking for advancement, a raise, so to speak, go ahead - work for whomever you wish. However, if you steal what's mine, I'll bury you in the jungle next to Tomas. Now, down to business. It's my understanding that Mr. DiNapoli is an honorable man. I have no reason to doubt it. However, for the first transaction, I insist on having the 20 million dollars before the Italians get the merchandise. Money upfront, as the saying goes. If this arrangement is acceptable to Mr. DiNapoli, then I'll proceed. We'll have the money deposited in several of our accounts. When the deposits are confirmed the merchandise will be stored in the usual manner. Diego, Miguel, and Carlos will go to New York to handle the transaction. Diego, you will stay with the Italians until the merchandise is tested and DiNapoli is satisfied. Make it clear to DiNapoli that the first shipment is merely the beginning and larger shipments are available if he chooses. Your contact is Sanchez. He is making the arrangements with the Italians. You've met, of course."

Diego responds "Sanchez is a puto. I hate that pendejo."

"That's good, because before you come home I want you to kill him."

"My pleasure, Padrone."

"Our warehouse #10 in the Brooklyn Navy Yard will be at the disposal of the Italians for as long as they need. So, gentlemen, if there's nothing else, it's time for relaxation. I have friends for you to meet." He motions to the women, and they stop what they're doing and gather around the men. "Enjoy yourselves and have anything you want, but remember to treat these women tenderly or answer to me."

# CHAPTER 25

# DINAPOLI CALLS FULLER

Fuller is reporting for work, and as he walks to his office his phone rings. Caller ID says DN, DiNapoli is on the other end. Fuller hesitates and then answers. "What can I do for you, Richie?"

"How's it going, Fuller?"

"I guess it depends on what you want."

Richie laughs. "Alright, I'll get to the point. You gotta detective working for you named Rodriguez, is that right?"

"Yeah, transferred from Vegas. All the way from Vegas to Oceanview."

"Doesn't that seem strange from Vegas to a small town in Long Island?"

"Not to me, Richie. I was short-handed and they sent me this guy. I didn't have a choice. He was a disciplinary problem according to Vegas PD., so now I'm stuck with him. Why all the questions, Richie."

"Why, cause something ain't right with this guy. He's harassing Sanchez, and this deal better not get fucked up. Rodriguez is sniffing around, asking questions and I want him to back off. That's where you come in, Fuller."

"Careful with the names, Richie."

"Don't worry, Fuller. I'm on the café phone. Stupid ass feds been trying to bug this phone forever. We're ok."

Fuller offers, "I got a missing person case I can put him on, that should keep him busy."

"I don't give a shit how you do it. Just keep him away from Sanchez."

"Sanchez is a piece of shit."

"Yeah, he is a piece of shit, but Delacruz won't do business with anybody else but him, at least on this deal. Stay focused, Fuller. After this deal is done we'll all be walking around with fuck you money. You can retire to a nice island somewhere and drink pina coladas all day and bang broads half your age all night."

"Ok, Richie. I'll take care of it."

"Yeah, I know you will. It's time to earn your money. Keep your cops, especially this fucking Rodriguez, away from Sanchez."

# CHAPTER 26

# GETTING TO KNOW YOU

Fuller calls Rodriguez into his office. Rodriguez enters and sits down. Fuller says, "We never had a real face-to-face talk since you got here, Detective. So how do you like Oceanview so far?"

"I like it. It's quiet."

"Don't let the quiet fool you. We get a lot of cases out here. Assholes commit crimes in the boroughs then come out here to hide out." Fuller does air quotes with his fingers for effect. "Coming from Vegas, this must bore you to tears. What made you choose Long Island?"

"I didn't, someone else picked it for me."

"That's right detective, your captain called me. Captain. . . I forgot his name."

"Steiner," Rodriguez fills in the blank.

"That's right, Steiner. He told me you were a disciplinary problem. You wanna explain?"

"Sure. You see Sergeant, I'm not subtle when it comes to police work, and I guess that pissed off my superiors."

"What do you mean subtle?"

"Well Sergeant, if I need to bury a foot in somebody's ass to get what I need, I bury the foot. It's that simple."

"Well, before you start that shit in Oceanview, make sure you check with me first. I'll decide who's ass you put your foot in. The folks in Oceanview don't appreciate aggressive policing. As long as they feel safe, we try not to expose them to the underbelly of law enforcement. Have you toured the town yet? People pay millions for their homes; let's not give them cause for concern. So how long have you been a cop?"

"About fourteen years, the last nine in Vegas."

"Where were you before Vegas?"

"I was in Florida and Arizona."

"Did you work big cases in those states, Detective?"

"Sure, we had some good cases. A lot of 'em were drug cases. The biggest case was a meth distribution case in Arizona."

"I'm sure you worked with the DEA in those drug cases."

"Yeah, sure. We collaborated. You know how it works."

Fuller leans back in his chair and asks, "So, you know people in the DEA?"

"Some. It's been awhile since I spoke to them."

Fuller is eying Rodriguez suspiciously, and after a while, he asks, "What made you become a cop?"

"It was either law enforcement or football, I think I made the right choice."

There is silence in the room, then Fuller says, "Alright detective, I'm gonna give you a case. It's a missing person case—her grandmother reported her missing. Here's the file, look it over." "Her name is Evelyn Lynch."

Fuller slides the file across the desk, and Rodriguez picks it up and flips through the pages.

"This girl has been missing for one week and I'm just getting the file now?"

"What do you want me to do, Rodriguez? I'm short detectives. Do you want the case or not?"

"Yeah, I'll take the case."

Rodriguez gets up and opens the door. He turns back and says to Fuller, "One week and we're here jerking off."

"Easy, Rodriguez. Don't forget who your boss is."

"Yeah, sure," Rodriguez replies and closes the door.

# CHAPTER 27

# EVELYN'S GRANDMOTHER

The next morning Rodriguez drives to the grandmother's house. The house is on a tree-lined street in a middle-class neighborhood. It's a midcentury brownstone with a brick exterior and nicely maintained landscaping. The grandmother's name is Janet Cooper. Rodriguez rings the bell; the voice on the intercom is loud and strong.

"Who is it?"

"I'm Detective Rodriguez. I'm here about your granddaughter."

"Ok, just a minute." Rodriguez looks around the neighborhood. It's a blue-collar area, well kept but by no means affluent. The door opens slightly and a tall grey-haired woman in her late sixties asks, "Do you have an ID, Officer?"

"Of course," Rodriguez responds and he shows her his badge and ID. The woman motions him inside to one of the rear two apartments.

As they walk to the apartment she says, "I had to move down here some years ago, the steps were too much for me. Besides, when my husband George died, our granddaughter moved in with me 'cause the apartments are bigger down here." They both sit down and the woman asks if he would like a cup of coffee. Rodriguez declines and takes a pad and pencil from his inside jacket pocket.

He says "Mrs. Cooper, I just want to let you know we'll do everything we can to find Evelyn. Can you give me her full name?"

"Evelyn Lynch."

"No middle name or aliases."

"No, just Evelyn."

"When did you see her last?"

"Monday night, as she was leaving for work around six p.m."

"Where does she work?"

"Not sure. She never mentioned the name. The only thing she told me is that it's an upscale, very expensive Italian restaurant."

"Do you know the address, Mrs. Cooper? Anything you can tell me to help me find the place."

"Only that it's on Main Street by the library."

Rodriguez asks how far is that from here, and Mrs. Cooper replies "About 3 miles."

"You said it's an upscale place?"

"Yes. Evelyn told me that dinner for two could cost 100 to 150 dollars. I can't afford that. I think that's pretty upscale, don't you, Detective?"

Rodriguez nods and asks, "Is Evelyn in a relationship with anybody?"

"She never mentioned anybody, but kids have a lot of secrets these days. I pray nothing happened to her."

Rodriguez puts his hand on hers and says, "We'll do our best to find her. Do you know if Evelyn did any type of drugs or if she drank alcohol to excess?"

"No detective, not that I saw. She always came home after her shift. I'm so worried about her."

"Did she mention names of friends or wanting to take a trip somewhere out of town?"

"No, Detective." She said she had friends at work and sometimes they would go out but, like I said, she always came home."

"Do you mind if I take a look in her bedroom? I may find something with the restaurant's name on it."

"Sure, that's a good idea. It's back here."

They walk to a well-kept, neat room in the back of the apartment. Rodriguez looks around the room and sees a photograph that appears to be a college graduation picture. He asks if he can have the photo, and she replies "Yes." Rodriguez removes it from its frame and puts the 4x6 photo in his pocket. He searches the drawers of the night stand and bureau and finds a pipe and some drug paraphernalia and quickly removes it and puts it in his pocket.

He turns to Mrs. Cooper and says, "I'm done. I'll have to canvas the restaurants on Main Street till I find out where she works. It should be easier now that I have her picture."

"Thank you, Detective. Let me walk you out. Please find her. I'm alone and I miss her so much."

"Mrs. Cooper, I have one more question if you don't mind. Evelyn's parents, where are they?"

"My daughter died years ago, and her father is an abusive drunk."

"We'll find her. I'll be in touch. Bye, Mrs. Cooper."

"Thank you, Detective. Goodbye."

He turns and walks down the steps as Mrs. Cooper closes the door. Rodriguez drives along Main Street and finds the library. He stops into two nearby restaurants and no one recognizes the woman in the picture. The third restaurant named "Loria's" is an upscale white table cloth establishment with a young good-looking wait staff, an amazing bar, murals of Italian landscapes and designer lighting. Rodriguez enters and is approached by a maître d' who says, "Sorry, sir. We open at 5 pm."

Rodriguez shows his badge and the maître d' asks, "How can I help you, officer?"

Rodriguez shows the maître d' her picture.

"This girl is missing and I'm looking for her. Her grandmother is worried sick. May I show her picture to some of the wait staff, maybe they know her? I was told she works at an upscale restaurant on Main Street."

"Yes, but please hurry. We're setting up for dinner."

"I get it. I'll keep it brief." The maître d' steps to the side and Rodriguez asks if he would have the wait staff gather in the middle of the room.

"It would be easier if I showed everyone the picture at one time, and then I'll be out of your hair."

The maître d' shouts, "Will the wait staff come to the middle of the room? The detective has a photo he would like you to look at."

The wait staff forms a line by the bar. "Is that everybody?"

The maître d' says, "Yes, unless you want the kitchen staff out here also."

"Yes, please. If you don't mind." The maitre'd sighs and hurries into the kitchen. The full staff is now assembled in front of the bar. The maître d', stressed, now walks away and checks on the table settings.

Rodriguez takes out the photo and walks up and down the line. "This girl is missing. Does anybody know her? She works at a restaurant. Does anybody know where?" One by one they say no. One girl makes eye contact with Rodriguez and discreetly tilts her head towards the back door once, twice, till Rodriguez understands the gesture. He puts the picture in his pocket and thanks everybody, including the maître d' who groans in response.

Rodriguez leaves the restaurant and walks around to the back. The girl is there waiting for him. She says to him, "Can I see the picture again?" Rodriguez shows her the photo. "That's Evelyn, Evelyn is her real name."

"What do you mean real name?"

"Detective, she doesn't work in a restaurant. She's a stripper. We work together at Ball Breakers. Her stripper name is Candy Willow. That's all I know. Please keep me out of it. If this place finds out I'm a stripper, they'll can me, and the money's better here."

"Was she doing drugs at the club?"

"Once in a while when she could get 'em. She hangs out with a bunch of assholes and really messed up people. I gotta get back, I'm gone too long."

"If anything else comes to mind you have my number," and he hands her his card. He asks, "What is your name?"

"Susan. I gotta get back." She begins to walk to the restaurant when Rodriguez asks, "About those messed up people—can you give me a name?" Susan walks back to him, gets closer and says—"Antonio Sanchez."

# CHAPTER 28

# THE CONFRONTATION

Sanchez is at home drinking and watching a ballgame when his phone rings. He recognizes the number as Rodriguez's. and he ignores the call. The phone continues to ring, then he picks up the phone and shouts "What?!"

Rodriguez asks "Where are you?"

"I'm in my house, why?"

"Stay there."

"Why should I? You can't tell me what to do."

"Cause I'm taking a field trip out to your hangout tonight and I don't want you there or I'll embarrass you in front of your crew."

Sanchez asks "Why are you going there anyway?"

Rodriguez replies, "I'm curious. Stay home, Sanchez."

Sanchez slams the phone down.

Antonio is angry and he calls Felix who answers, "Where are you, man? We're waiting for you."

Sanchez responds, "I ain't coming tonight, but I need you to do something for me."

"What is it, Antonio?"

"I want you to get some of the players together, three or four. I want you to fuck somebody up for me."

"What, who?"

"His name is Rodriquez. He's a big dude, black hair, dark eyes, ain't never been there before, you'll know when you see him. Be careful, he carries a gun so make sure he doesn't see it coming. Get some of your junkie friends together, you know that crack head Angel, Freddie and that crazy Irish guy Tommy—he's a fucking psycho—tell 'em there's a grand each in it. Just hurt him, and one more thing—tell him to stay away from Antonio Sanchez. There's a grand in it for you. You gonna do it?"

"Sure, Antonio, sure."

<hr>

The black Lincoln drives to Ball Breakers and parks on the side of the club. Rodriguez walks into Ball Breakers and all eyes are on him. He looks like he doesn't belong, and nobody knows him. He walks to the bar, orders a beer and puts ten bucks down. As he's drinking his beer he looks around the room and notices the men playing pool. Felix catches his eye and Rodriguez turns back to the bar. Felix whispers to his friends. "Yo, I think that's the dude. We'll get him outside and bring the sticks. Hurt him real bad."

Rodriguez motions to the bartender and he walks over. Rodriguez shows the bartender the picture and asks, "You know her?"

"Yeah, that's Evelyn, but she hasn't been here and I can't reach her, so I stopped trying. You look like a cop."

"Yeah, I'm a cop, and I'd rather not flash a badge in this joint if you know what I mean. Her grandmother reported her missing. When did you see her last?"

"I think it was Monday night. She went home in a cab. I think she was sick or stoned or something. A couple of the regular assholes told me they put her in a cab."

"Assholes. Who are these assholes?"

"A guy named Sanchez and this guy Felix. A couple of douchebags."

"Let me ask you something—how long have you been working here?"

"About seven years."

"In all those seven years, how many cabs have you seen in this neighborhood?"

The bartender thinks for a minute and says, "Now that you said it, I ain't never seen one. They don't come down this way."

Rodriguez nods and asks, "You got cameras in this place?"

The bartender laughs. "If we put cameras in this place we wouldn't have any customers."

Rodriguez points to the locked door in the back by the men's room and asks, "What's in there?"

"I don't know. I don't have a key."

"Who does?"

"Sanchez, but you didn't hear it from me."

Rodriguez finishes his beer and slides 10 dollars to the bartender and says, "Keep the change."

"There is no change, the beer is 15 bucks."

"Fifteen, wonderful." He places another 10 on the bar.

"You want change?"

"Nah, keep it. Oh, one more thing. The guys you mentioned—Sanchez and Felix. I know what Sanchez looks like. Is Felix in here now? Just a yes or no."

"Yeah, he's the skinny ugly one with the shitty goatee."

"Thanks. Men's room back there?"

"Yeah. just before the exit."

Rodriguez walks to the back and out the unlocked exit door. He looks around and sees what looks like a warehouse building with two men standing outside. He looks up and notices two cameras, one facing Ball Breakers. Rodriguez approaches the men.

"You guys work here?"

"Yeah."

"Is this place 24/7?"

"Yep, unfortunately. Are you a cop or something?"

"Yeah, looking for a missing person." He gestures to the cameras. "Do they work?"

One of the men says, "I don't know. Ask the boss. He's inside, but I gotta tell you he's in a shitty mood."

"So am I."

One of the men uses a key card to let Rodriguez in. "Go straight back, his office is right there," he says, pointing to the back.

Rodriguez walks to the back of the warehouse and, as he walks, forklifts and people are working and moving around him.

A worker approaches him and asks, "Can I help you?" Rodriguez shows his badge and says, "I'm looking for the boss.'

"Keep walking straight back. You can't miss him."

Rodriguez finds the 'Boss' in a dingy office with stained walls, a wall calendar that's two months behind and a dirty and dusty Mr. Coffee machine. Not looking up from his computer, the boss says, "What can I do for you?"

Rodriguez shows his badge and says, "I'm Detective Rodriguez. I'm searching for a missing girl. Do those cameras outside work?"

The boss is a short pale and pudgy man with thick glasses, thin hair and a lazy eye. He replies, "Yeah, they work, otherwise they'd be no damn good. Ain't that right, Detective?"

"Do they record to tape or live stream?"

"I don't know. They're right there all nice and neat. My security guy is anal about shit like that."

"Can I see last Monday night?"

"Not now, I'm busy, up to my ass in work."

"I see. If I called OSHA, Immigration and got a warrant, would that make you less busy?"

"Look, detective, I got 30 guys out there just on this shift. Half of 'em are ex-cons, some are doing drugs and the rest are probably sleeping somewhere in this building. I can't watch everybody, and you're just adding to my shit to-do list—you get it?"

"Yeah, I get it, but it's important to her grandmother." Rodriguez sees a picture on the desk of a family. "Nice picture. Is that your family?"

The boss says, "Thank you, Detective. My wife Jennie passed a few years back—cancer took her, but she fought. Boy did she fight; beat the odds. The genius doctors gave her 6 to 8 months—she hung around for two years. That handsome guy is me and my daughters, Allison and Sara. They're all I got and I love 'em to death. In medical school, both of 'em."

"You must be proud. I sure am. They're in medical school because they're smart."

"Look around you, Detective, what do you think they pay me here? They got scholarships—both of 'em—damn right I'm proud."

"I'm sorry about your wife. The girl I'm looking for is about the same age as your daughters. I promised her grandmother I'd find her. That tape would be a great help.""

The boss says, "Same age as my daughters, you said?"

"Yeah, she's about 25-26." The boss shakes his head and points to two cassettes and says, "Monday during the day and Monday night."

"Thanks. Is there any way I can watch in private?"

"Sure, I gotta make rounds, anyway." The boss points to the VCR on the desk and asks, "You know how to use it?"

"I think I can figure it out. If I see some evidence on the tape, can I take it?"

"Sure, don't worry about it."

"Thanks." The boss grabs a clipboard and leaves the office. Rodriguez hears him shout, "Everybody line up for attendance check. If anybody out there is smoking, put 'em out and get in here."

Rodriguez loads the tape and begins to watch, the back exit of Ball Breakers is grainy but visible on the screen. He goes through the tape. At 9:10 pm a man staggers out and pees against the wall of the club, obviously drunk. Rodriguez mutters to himself, "Nice move. There's a bathroom inside, asshole." At 10:10 a stripper who's half-naked and a male patron are taking a marijuana break. As he takes a drag on the joint she leans against him and rubs his crotch. They finish the joint and go back inside. At 10:20 a man leaves the club and he goes off camera range. A few minutes later a car comes into range and backs up to the rear door. The same man exits the car, opens the trunk and goes back inside. Rodriguez notices the man is using the private office that is used by Sanchez. Rodriguez continues to forward the tape. At 10:40, two men exit the club carrying what appears to be a heavy object wrapped in black garbage bags and taped all around. The men struggle with the bag and finally maneuver it into the trunk. The shorter man gets into the driver's seat and drives away. Approximately five minutes later, the taller man bolts from the office locks the door and runs out of camera range. Rodriguez is convinced that the taller man is Sanchez. He grabs both tapes and is leaving the warehouse when the boss intercepts him at the door.

"Find what you were looking for, Detective?"

"Yeah, thanks for helping out."

"Hope you find her."

Rodriguez goes back to Ball Breakers and tries the rear door to the mysterious office but it's locked. He uses a knife to jimmy the lock and the door opens.

The room smells of cheap perfume and stale beer. He looks around and notices white powder residue and empty beer bottles on the table. In the background, he hears music as the dancers perform on stage. He sees a row of lockers and attempts to open them, but he finds that some are locked and others are empty. One locker has been moved and is out of line with the others. Behind it is a wall safe. He photographs the room and the wall safe with his phone. He leaves the room the same way he came in and closes the door behind him. He walks back into the club and sits at the bar. The bartender comes over and says, "I thought you left. Do you want another beer?"

"Not at fifteen dollars a pop I don't."

"The boss doesn't like when we buy back but this one on me."

"Thanks." He looks up at the dancers behind the bar and notices the differences between the two girls. He calls the bartender over and asks him, "The girl on this side of the stage, you know the girl next door type, what's her name?"

"Around here we call her Cinnamon."

"Cinnamon," Rodriguez says. He finishes his beer straight from the bottle, gets up, puts 10 dollars on the bar and walks to the door. He looks at Felix on the way out and it dawns on him that Felix is the other man on the tape. Felix and three of his crew stop playing pool and follow Rodriguez out.

Rodriguez has his back to the club as he makes it to his car. The element of surprise was on the side of the thugs as the first blow strikes Rodriguez in the lower back. Stunned Rodriguez turns to see another pool cue coming for his head. He dodges and grabs the pool stick and smashes the base of it into the thug's nose which immediately gushes blood. Crazy Tommy who's been in and out of prison most of his life hits Rodriguez in his midsection with the end of the cue. Rodriguez hardly feels this due to his many hours in the gym. Tommy is surprised by this and it gives Rodriguez an opening to leverage the cue to flip Tommy to the concrete. Tommy's head hits the floor with a thud. Rodriguez turns his attention to the two remaining men and one pulls a knife on Rodriguez. He lunges at him and Rodriguez uses the pool cue as a club and disarms the thug. At that moment the other thug strikes Rodriguez to the back of the head. The blow stuns Rodriguez and he is struck again as he slides to the floor against his car. At that point the parking lot is spinning and the men begin to kick him. Rodriguez is still conscious as Felix sticks his face two inches from his and says, "Stay the fuck away from Sanchez." The combination of Felix's intensely bad breath and adrenaline in Rodriguez causes him to grab Felix by the neck and squeeze. Felix is surprised by how much strength he has left and he tries to get Rodriguez's hands from his throat. The next blow to his head causes him to let go of Felix and go into a state of semi-consciousness. He lies in the deserted parking lot for half an hour.

A voice begins to wake him and he pulls himself up. He feels warm blood on the back of his head. His ribs are aching and he's almost on his feet. He feels two arms around him trying to help him up. The same voice comes into focus, "I'm gonna call an ambulance." Through the fog he sees the outline of a woman. It's the dancer Cinnamon.

He says, "No ambulance."

Cinnamon replies, "You may have a concussion. You should get to the hospital."

Rodriguez ignores her and turns and opens the car door. He says, "Thanks for the help, Cinnamon."

She closes the door to his car and asks, "You sure you can drive?"

"Yeah, I'll be alright. Thanks again." He drives off.

# CHAPTER 29

# THE REAL FULLER

Fuller is shaving, the mirror is steamed up. A young girl comes from behind him wraps her arms around him and whispers "When you're done I'll be waiting in bed."

"No, you won't. Get dressed and take your money, it's on the bed."

"Just one more time, daddy, then I'll go."

"Get lost! I spent enough money for one day. Now take the cash and get the fuck out."

"I've been a bad girl, don't you want to discipline me?" Fuller stops shaving and throws the blade into the sink. He grabs the girl's clothes and money and throws them into the hall. He grabs the girl by the hair and says, "I told you to get the fuck out." He drags her into the hall and slams the door. The girl is shouting and banging on the door.

"I'm telling everybody what kind of a prick you are and how you like to play with underage girls, you motherfucker! That's right, Fuller, I know you're a cop."

The door opens and Fuller pulls her back in. "Listen to me, you little junkie bitch. If you ever tell anybody about me or mention my name again I'll kill you real bad. You'll wind up just another dead hooker. Now get your shit and leave. Don't force me to hurt you. You understand me?" The girl doesn't respond, so Fuller grabs her by the neck and says, "You got it?"

The girl nods furiously. He opens the door and pushes her into the hall. She picks up her clothes, sobbing loudly. A door opens and an old woman peeks through the opening and sees the young girl. She asks "Are you hurt, child?"

The girl says "No, go back inside." The door closes.

# CHAPTER 30

# THE SCORE IS EVEN

Sanchez hasn't heard from Rodriguez since the beating and figures Rodriguez got the message. On the third day, his phone rings and it's Rodriguez. He ignores it. On the third try he picks up. Rodriguez says, "We need to talk."

"About what?"

"About money. You want me to back off, it's gonna cost you."

"How much?"

"Fifty grand, and you won't hear from me again."

"Fifty thousand's a lot of money."

"Yeah, and I know you got it—you're dealing drugs out of that club you hang out in. So fifty grand—and I want it tonight. Ten 'o' clock at the spot."

Sanchez arrives at the diner late as usual. Rodriguez is sitting at the usual table. Sanchez slides into the booth and looks at Rodriguez and says, "I guess you met my crew" with a smirk on his face.

Rodriguez responds, "Yeah I was pissing blood for a few days."

"Wow, they really fucked you up. I heard you put up a fight. You think you're a real tough guy, don't you, puto?"

"You got my money?"

At that point the waitress comes to the table and says, "Good evening, gentlemen. Would you like the usual bagel and coffee for the nice man, and nothing for Mr. Personality?"

Sanchez barks at her, "Get lost, bitch!"

Rodriguez asks the waitress to give them a minute, and then asks again, "Where's the money?"

"Give me a few days I'll get it. So I give you the cash and then what happens?"

Rodriguez is staring at Sanchez and says, "What happens? This happens." The speed at which Rodriguez grabs Sanchez by the collar of his jacket, dragging him across the table, totally catches Sanchez off guard. He's pinned to the floor with Rodriguez's fist in his throat. Rodriguez tells him, "If you ever get your junkie friends on me again I'll kill the whole bunch of you." Sanchez is gasping for air and he punches at Rodriguez but his hand is swatted away. Sanchez's eyes are bulging as Rodriguez continues, "You just made this personal, maricon. I'll be in touch." Before he loosens his grip he pats him down and finds a gun and states, "I'll keep this," as he gets on his feet. He hands the waitress a twenty dollar bill and leaves the diner. Sanchez is on the floor trying to catch his breath, coughing and cursing Rodriguez, his eyes tearing and bloodshot.

The waitress approaches Sanchez and asks, "You sure I can't get you anything?" to which Sanchez responds, "Fuck you!"

---

Later that week, Rodriguez is on his way to the precinct when his phone rings and he answers. "Good morning, Sarge." McMahon sounds annoyed.

"Good morning, my ass. I got a call a few minutes ago from Captain Steiner. Do you know who that is?"

"Sure, he signed my transfer papers."

"Well, Rodriguez, it seems Fuller called him. He's claiming you threw Sanchez a beating at some coffee shop in front of about ten witnesses."

"Ten? It was about three. The place is a dive—nobody goes there."

"Don't crack wise, Rodriguez. I'm in no fucking mood. The bottom line is you gotta back off Sanchez."

"But Sarge, didn't you tell me to introduce myself?"

"I said to introduce yourself, not choke the guy out."

"So maybe I did get a little carried away, but that was a revenge beating. He sicced some of his playmates on me outside that strip club he hangs out in."

"Why am I finding out about this now? Assaulting an officer is serious shit."

"What about murder, Sarge, how serious is that?"

"Murder? What are you talking about?"

"About a week ago Fuller gave me a missing persons case. A young girl by the name of Evelyn Lynch. Her grandmother reported her missing. What her grandmother didn't know was that she was working as a stripper where Sanchez hangs out. I went out there to interview the people that work there. I spoke to the bartender, and he told me that Sanchez and a guy named Felix were the last people to see her alive. Sanchez told him she was drunk and they put her in a cab."

"So what do you think happened, Rodriguez?"

"I think the cab story is bullshit, Sarge. I looked around outside the place and I saw a building across the street with cameras. One of the cameras caught a piece of the strip club exit. There's a room in the back of the club by the exit and only Sanchez has the key. On the tape there's two people carrying a black garbage bag out of that room. The bag looks heavy, they're struggling with it and finally they get the bag into the trunk of a car."

"And Rodriguez, you think there was a body in that bag?"

"I think it's the missing girl, Evelyn Lynch."

"Shit, Rodriguez. You think Sanchez killed her?"

"I don't know who killed her, but one of the people is his size and body type and I'll bet the other guy is Sanchez's pet chihuahua, Felix."

"Can you see any faces on this tape?"

"No. Sarge. It's dark and the film is grainy."

"How did you get this tape? I hope you didn't take it without permission."

"No, the manager of the warehouse gave it to me."

"Did he give it up voluntarily?"

"Yeah, he did, Sarge. I noticed some family pictures on his desk. It was his wife and two daughters. I told him his daughters are about the same age as the missing girl. I guess he felt he had to help under those circumstances."

"Whatever works. I guess for right now keep the tape in a safe place. We can't make a move on Sanchez yet."

"But Sarge, it's a murder rap. We could use it for information on DiNapoli."

"I appreciate your enthusiasm, Detective, but based on what you just told me, there is no murder rap. If we pick him up now and he's involved with DiNapoli, we'll have nothing. You can't see anybody's face on the tape, it's the bartender's word, no witnesses and nobody saw them leave together. Leave Sanchez alone for now. Let him think he won. When we get him on the drug rap we'll push for a murder conviction on top of it."

# CHAPTER 31

# READY TO MOVE

Richie and his crew are at the social club playing cards. The phone rings and Dom picks it up. "It's Antonio, give me Richie."

Dom yells over to Richie, "Hey Richie. It's Sanchez."

Richie throws his cards down and says "Now what?" He goes to the phone. "Yeah, what's up Antonio?"

"We're ready to move."

"Come to Brooklyn tomorrow at two. I'll buy you a coffee." Richie hangs up and returns to the table and says, "We're on, gentlemen."

---

It's 2:20 the following day. Richie and his crew are seated at a table in a corner of the social club. Antonio Sanchez is twenty minutes late, and Dom looks at his watch and is growing inpatient. At 2:30, Sanchez walks in and heads toward the table. Richie puts up his hand and says, "Hold it Antonio. Primo, check him. Sorry Antonio, house rules."

Primo frisks Antonio and finds a 9mm gun and a straight edge razor and says, "That's it, boss. He's clean."

Dom sees the razor and says "Hey Primo, let's see that." Primo hands the razor to Dom.

Dom opens the Razor and tests the blade on the back of his hand. Without looking up he says "You kept me waiting again. Are you ever on time for anything?"

Sanchez replies, "Traffic, couldn't help it."

"I like this blade. I see you keep it sharp."

"Yeah, otherwise it's just a toy."

Dom says,"Back in the day when I was coming up, it was my weapon of choice when I needed to be quiet. Know what I mean? I like it. It's old school, black handle diamond in the middle. Real nice." Dom turns to Primo and adds, "You could learn something about tradition; it's what's missing today—finesse. You like it, Primo?"

Primo replies, "It's ok, but I prefer these," and he shows Dom his large hands and a 45-caliber Glock from a shoulder holster. Dom is still admiring the razor, and he asks Antonio, "Did you ever use it?"

"Yeah when I was in Colombia, working for Delacruz."

"You mean Colombian neckties and all that shit?"

"Yeah, that's what snitches get in Colombia."

Dom says "Badass Sanchez, you wanna give me a Colombian necktie?"

Sanchez stares at Dom and says, "No, but keep fuckin' with me and …"

Richie steps in mid-conversation and says, "Enough of this shit, we got business."

Richie turns to Primo and says, "Thanks, Primo. Now we got business to discuss." Primo gets up and walks to a different table. Richie asks Sanchez, "So what's the word from Delacruz?

"The first shipment is 1500 pounds of merchandise, the cost to you is 20 million. After that you decide when and how much. Mr. Delacruz only asks that your next purchase happens within ninety days of the first fifteen hundred pounds. Delacruz is willing to give you an exclusive to sell you his product, but you gotta buy more before ninety days is up or he goes to the competition."

"How do I know he won't sell to the competition, anyway?"

"You don't, Richie, but if you don't buy more, it's guaranteed he's going somewhere else, and you'll be out. There's a warehouse at the Brooklyn Navy Yard. It's number 10. It's at your disposal - compliments of Delacruz. Use it to test the product or store it for a few days. Delacruz wants you to be happy. Your contact will be Diego Vargas—treat him with respect. He used to be Delacruz's enforcer but now he's his business manager. He enjoys killing—you hear me Dom—so be careful."

"See how scared I am, asshole."

"Knock it off, Dom. Go ahead, Sanchez."

"Five crates each containing three hundred pounds of merchandise will be waiting for you. How will you transport it?"

"In the back of a garbage truck, how else?"

"That's original. Richie says we'll keep the truck in the warehouse for a few days. When the time is right we'll drive it to Long Island City."

Sanchez reaches into his pocket and takes out his cell phone. He shows the screen to Richie. On it are 10 account numbers. "Mr. Delacruz requests that you place two million dollars in each of ten banks. Don't worry. These deposits can't be traced. Your money and where it came from is protected. Mr. Delacruz doesn't take chances when it comes to his money."

"So let me get this straight—it's money before product?

"That's the only way he'll do business. It's your decision. You can walk away if you don't like it."

"So Richie, when do I get paid?"

"It depends."

"Depends on what, Richie?"

"What's Delacruz paying you?"

"No offense, but that's between Delacruz and me."

Richie thinks for a minute and says, "Ok, Antonio. That's fair enough. Now answer me this—who was in that garbage bag you and one of your fucking friends threw in the back of your car?"

"How the fuck do you know about that, Richie? "Were you following me? Dom says,"I was. Richie don't do that no more."

"The question hasn't been answered—who was in that bag?"

Antonio nervously answers, "A stripper. She won't be missed."

Richie looks around the table at the men gathered there and asks, "Did you kill her?"

"No, it wasn't me. It was one of the guys I hang out with."

"Does this guy, this fucking hero, have a name?"

"His name is Felix. They were doing drugs together and he wanted some pussy—you know—for the drugs, and she wouldn't give it up."

Richie is leaning forward in his chair staring at Antonio with his hand up to his chin. He opens his other hand in front of Dom and says, "Give me your razor."

"What're you gonna do?" Antonio is visibly scared.

Richie takes the blade and opens it. He holds the razor close to Antonio's face.

"Back in the day, I did my share. I did what I had to do, but killing a woman—that's a line I wouldn't cross." Richie moves the razor closer to Antonio's face. "If I took this razor right now and cut your fucking throat it would be a soul for a soul." Antonio is staring at the blade as Richie moves it back and forth in front of his face. He asks Dom, "Hey Dom, would this be the first time I killed somebody in this place?"

"No, Richie it wouldn't."

Antonio shudders. "But Richie, I didn't kill her, it was Felix."

"It doesn't matter. God wants a soul, a soul for a soul." Richie is still holding the blade and is staring at Antonio. He finally folds the blade and gives it back to Dom. "Tell Delacruz he's got a deal, we'll wire the money soon. Maxie, take care of it. Antonio, get with Maxie and give him the numbers." Sanchez lets out a sigh of relief. Richie adds, "If the merchandise is like the stuff we sampled, we're gonna do a lot of business. As for you getting paid, when the deal is done I'll pay you two million dollars, like we agreed." One more thing before you go, Sanchez. I was told you and that hero friend of yours dumped that girl's body in one of my scrap yards without my permission. I need you for this deal, otherwise you and that piece of shit friend of yours would be in the back of one of my trucks." Richie motions to Primo. "Empty his gun and give it back to him. Get your shit from Primo and get the fuck out of here."

Sanchez opens the door to leave and, as he does, the church bells from across the street begin to ring.

A member of Richie's crew approaches the table. Richie waves him over and the man whispers in Richie's ear and motions towards the storeroom in the back. Richie nods and says to Dom, "Let's go." Both men walk to a store room in back of the social club. Primo leaves his table and joins them. In the room are two refrigerators that fill the room with a low pitched hum. Bright fluorescent lights cast an annoying blue cast throughout the room. Tied to a chair beneath one of these lights is Joey Palumbo. He's in and out of reality, having taken a more than usual dose of heroin. Joey is one of Richie's dealers who broke the golden rule of drug dealing—do not use what you sell. The men enter the room and close the door behind them. Richie pulls up a chair and sits directly in front of Joey. He calls out, "Joey, Joey wake up." He slaps Joey's face and continues to call, "Joey, it's Richie, wake the fuck up. Let's go, Joey." Joey comes to his senses and sees it's Richie. He's sleepy and trying to focus. He realizes it's Richie and he panics. "Richie, I'm sorry I'm back on the shit. I'll get straight Richie—give me a chance."

"I'm tired of giving you chances, you fucking mook—this one's number three. You know me and your old man go back 20 years at least. When he went to prison, he begged me to bring you into my crew. He knew you were a fuck up, Joey. He knew you couldn't make it on your own. He begged me, Joey, and I gave in 'cause your old man was like a brother to me."

"Richie, I'm a good earner. I always was."

"You were, Joey, and then you started using my shit. What did I tell you when I took you in? I told you 'don't use what you sell.' Ain't that right, Joey?"

Joey begins to nod out again, and Richie calls him but there's no answer from Joey. Richie gives him the back of his hand across his face. "Wake the fuck up, Joey. I'm talking to you." Dom and Primo who are standing behind Joey glance at each other. They're witnessing Richie at his worst. "When you use what you sell, it costs me 'cause it's my drugs, Joey. You're stealing from me. Do you know that?"

"Please Richie, give me just one more chance."

Richie looks at Dom and nods, "So you want one more chance, Joey? Hey, Dom, should we give him one more chance?" Joey begins sobbing and begging Richie, but it falls on deaf ears. Dom has a syringe filled with a lethal dose of heroin. Joey sees it and begins to scream. Primo covers Joey's mouth with his big hand as Dom stabs Joey in the neck with the syringe. Joey is kicking at Richie as Richie moves his chair back and watches Joey as he convulses and goes limp in the chair. Primo says, "I think he's dead, boss." Richie takes a handkerchief, wipes his hands and says, "Say hello to your old man. Hey, Dom, get a few of the boys and dump this piece of shit."

# CHAPTER 32

# MCMAHON MEETS EBERSOLE

McMahon is in her office when her phone rings. It's Captain Ebersole from Brooklyn organized crime. "How are you, Sergeant McMahon? I've got some news that'll make your day. We have new evidence linking Primo to the murder of Sallie Boy several months back. I'm giving you a call cause I know you DEA guys are working on a trafficking case involving the DiNapoli family. We have a tape that puts Primo at the scene. His face is clear—there's no doubt it's him. We made some prints from the tape, and we're thinking we can use the evidence to turn him against DiNapoli. There's a phone in the Social Club, an old school payphone that we can't seem to tap remotely. Maybe we can get Primo to bug the phone and different areas of the club. The only problem we're having is getting Primo alone long enough. Do you want in?"

Sergeant McMahon responds. "Sure I want in, and I can help you with getting Primo alone. Every Wednesday DiNapoli has a family meeting at his Social Club. He doesn't let Primo in on the meeting, and as it turns out Primo goes to the aquarium—we can grab him there."

"How do you know that, Sergeant?"

"Let's just say it comes from a reliable source and leave it at that."

"Ok, Sergeant, I get it. Today's Monday. Can you get here tomorrow?"

"I'll get on a flight tonight."

"Ok, great. We're at 17 Water Street in downtown Manhattan. When you get here I'll introduce you to the team and I'll go over the evidence with you." "That's good, Captain. See you tomorrow."

McMahon arrives at the organized crime headquarters. The entrance to the building is a plain stone facade with two glass doors. Written on one of the doors is "NYPD Organized Crime Unit —Brooklyn Division." McMahon wonders to herself why they would advertise. She goes in and notices the lack of security. Sitting at a desk is a man in uniform reading a newspaper. He looks up, hands McMahon a clipboard and says, "Sign in and go through the metal detector. That guy on the end will tell you what to do."

McMahon shows her badge and says, "I'm a Sergeant with the Las Vegas DEA and I'm armed."

The man answers, "You gotta check the gun, cuffs or whatever is on this list," and he shows McMahon a list of prohibited items.

You're telling me nobody in this building carries a weapon?"

"They do, but they work here. You don't." He grabs a plastic tub from the floor and puts it on the desk "Put your stuff in here." The man gives her a visitor pass and says, "You need to wear this while you're in the building. Take your stuff to that guy and go through the metal detector."

The other man takes the tub and puts it on the other side of the metal detector as she goes through. He asks, "Who are you here to see?"

"Capt. Danny Ebersole."

"I couldn't help overhearing you're from Vegas."

"Yes I am."

"I go there a lot. Last time I was there, I beat the crap out of those slots and took 'em for eighteen hundred."

"A whole eighteen hundred—let me know the next time you go. I'll let the casinos know there's a high roller in town, just as a heads up."

The man just looks at McMahon, not knowing how to respond. McMahon adds, "Listen, I wanna keep my gun. Who makes that call?"

"Ebersole. He's in charge of the building. I gotta ask him."

"Would you, please? I'm already late."

The man slowly and purposely picks up the phone and dials, and after a while says, "Hi, Captain. I got a woman down here who says her name is McMahon, and she wants to keep her gun." There's a pause. "Ok, Captain, I'll give it to her. Thanks."

The man hands her the gun and says, "Go to the 9th floor. He's in room 9F." McMahon says thanks and walks past the man to the elevators.

McMahon walks into room 9F. The room is busy with agents, people at computers and uniformed NYPD officers. Captain Ebersole is a 30 year veteran of the NYPD. He worked homicide, vice, and finally ended up in the organized crime unit. In his 30 years of service he's been shot, stabbed and beaten up, he's due to retire but his love of the job keeps him going. He's gathered around a table with a few agents. They're gesturing and talking loudly, and the conversation is dominated by Ebersole. He looks past the agents and sees McMahon, excuses himself, and comes to greet her. "Hi Sergeant, I'm Danny Ebersole," he says, extending his hand.

McMahon replies, "Did you hire those guys downstairs?"

"Well, good morning to you, too."

"I'm sorry, Captain. I'm a little short on patience this morning. I'm Elizabeth McMahon."

"Nice to meet you," he says, and they shake hands. "Come over. I'll introduce you to the team." They walk over to the table where there's agents waiting for Ebersole and he makes the introductions. "This is the team you'll be working with tomorrow. This is agent Alex Ruiz—he'll be driving the car. This handsome gentleman is agent Johnny Powell—he'll cover Primo to make sure he doesn't get out of line. In the backup car we got agent Anna Flores and John Harris—you'll meet them later. Sergeant, come into my office. I wanna show you the pictures we got." Ebersole takes a manila envelope from the top drawer of his desk; he turns it over and six pictures land on this desk. "Look we got six shots off that tape. Primo's face is clear in four out of the six."

McMahon asks, "Where did you get these?"

"There's one building at the end of the street among the abandoned buildings in that alley. The only occupied floor of that building was used to shoot pornography. The cameraman heard the commotion in the alley, turned his camera out the window, and got the murder on tape. Turns out a few of the people in these films were under-age." "Kiddie porn? "No, but borderline. His lawyer traded the pictures for less jail time. We don't know who ordered the hit. There's no doubt it's Primo."

"Let me see those pictures." McMahon looks at the pictures and says, "There's no question that's Primo. These are pretty brutal."

"Yeah, they sure are. Primo breaks his neck then shoots him in the head twice."

McMahon asks, "What was Sallie Boy doing there in the first place?"

"Don't know. Maybe Primo can tell us. Let's go outside and talk about the details with the rest of the team."

They approach the rest of the team and Ebersole gives them their instructions. "Tomorrow morning we'll be at the Social Club at 10 a.m. Primo normally gets there between 10:30 and 11. We'll follow Primo to the aquarium or wherever he goes. The cars will leapfrog to avoid being spotted. When he gets to where he's going, Agent Flores and Harris in the backup car will bring him to you, McMahon. Remember, if he goes to the aquarium there may be families with children there so be careful. Catch him off guard, and bring him to McMahon. If he agrees to turn on DiNapoli, we'll drive him to the safehouse and brief him. If not you've got to take him into custody. Be careful. He's a killer."

McMahon says, "I wanna be the one that talks to him."

Ebersole asks,"Any objections?" It's quiet, and nobody speaks up. "Ok then. McMahon will do the talking. But remember, Agent Ruiz is in charge. Ok, people, let's break and meet up here tomorrow morning at 8 a.m."

Ebersole turns to McMahon and asks,"Do you have plans for dinner? Would you like to join me? I know a great Italian place nearby."

"Thanks, Captain, but I'm exhausted. I just wanna get back to my hotel and sleep. Any other time I would take you up on it."

"I understand, Sergeant. Get some rest. Tomorrow we'll do this thing."

"Good night, Captain."

# CHAPTER 33

# PRIMO'S DAY OF RECKONING

Primo is driving Richie and Dom to the Social Club in Brooklyn. He doesn't notice the two cars parked near the Club as he drops off his passengers. Richie says, "Primo, take the day off. We got a late meeting tonight, so take the day off and go say hello to Orca. Enjoy yourself." Richie and Dom chuckle as they enter the Social Club. "Thanks, boss," Primo shouts.

Primo is happy because he gets to spend time at his favorite place, the Brooklyn Aquarium.

Primo arrives at the Aquarium, exits his car and fast walks to the ticket booth excitedly with money in hand. A car parks next to his, and a man and a woman in suits exit. The other car with McMahon and the two other agents goes around to the back of the parking lot. The two agents approach Primo from either side. Agent Flores shows her badge and says, "Come with us, keep your hands at your side. There's kids here, let's not have a bad scene." Agent Harris puts his gun against Primo's back and says, "Make a fuss, and I'll put a hole in your kidney. Move to the back—somebody wants to talk to you." They reach the car, and McMahon opens the door. Harris pats Primo down and removes Primo's weapon. Harris looks at the size of the gun and says, "What do you do with this fucking cannon?"

Primo responds, "Give it back and I'll show you."

Agent Harris says, "Get in the car, asshole." A female voice adds, "Get in, Primo."

Primo gets in beside McMahon and asks "Who are you?"

"I'm Sargent McMahon with the DEA. This is Agent Ruiz and Agent Powell; they're with the organized crime unit. They're here to make sure you're polite."

"So, Mr. Delicato. Delicato, isn't that 'delicate' in Italian?"

"Yeah, so what?"

"So how's Sallie Boy doing? It wasn't too delicate the way you killed him."

Primo says "Sallie who?"

"Sallie Boy. Somebody broke his neck."

"Too bad for Sallie Boy, but I don't know shit about that. Can I go now, is that it?"

"No Primo, that's not it. Here, open it," and she hands Primo the manila envelope.

Primo asks, "What's this?"

"Open it, Primo."

"Why, what 's inside?"

"Open it and find out." He opens the envelope, and the pictures fall out of the envelope and onto his lap.

Primo picks up the pictures, goes through them and hands them back to McMahon.

McMahon says, "You were thorough that day, Primo. You didn't leave any clues."

Primo stares straight ahead with no emotion, and asks "Where did you get these?"

"There were cameras in the alleyway, but none of them were working. At the end of the alley there's an abandoned building, abandoned except for one floor. You wanna know what they did on that floor, Primo?"

"What?"

"Porn."

"So what? It ain't against the law."

"Depends on what state you're in. But you know what's against the law everywhere? "Using minors for porn."

Primo hangs his head and says "Fuck."

"Yeah, fuck, you piece of shit. You knew there were minors in there and you didn't say shit."

"No, I thought it was the regular stuff."

"It seems the scumbag that was operating the camera heard a commotion in the alleyway, turned his camera out the window, and guess what—his lawyer just traded these pictures for less jail time for the scumbag. That's good for the guy with the camera, but too bad for you, Primo. I read Sallie Boy's record and, to be honest, you did us all a favor. But murder is murder, and you gotta answer for it, Primo. How did you do it?" McMahon asks.

Agent Powell turns and looks at McMahon.

Primo answers, "You know."

"Yeah I know, but we wanna hear it from you. How did you know Sallie Boy was gonna be there? Did you follow him?"

"No, I waited for him."

McMahon asks, "Was DiNapoli behind the hit?"

"No, it was an open contract and I took it. I would have done it for free. I hated that prick. Everybody knew he liked to watch."

"Watch what?

"You know, porn. One of my associates told me he was gonna be there. I hid out in one of the doorways. When he got close I stepped out. I wanted him to see me face to face when I killed him. I wanted my face to be the last thing he saw before I snapped his neck."

Agent Powell again turns and looks at McMahon. McMahon looks back at Primo who's still staring straight ahead. Primo continues "When he saw me, he was fucking with me, and he said something that really pissed me off."

"What was that, Primo?"

"He said, 'What're you doing here, Primo? Looking for something to eat?'"

Powell turns to McMahon with a half smile on his face. McMahon says, "Go ahead, Primo."

Primo continues, "The dumb prick didn't realize he was about to die. I put my hands around his skinny neck and I broke his neck in less than five seconds. He didn't have time to reach for his gun. Fuck him."

"What happened next, Primo?"

"I held him there for a while to make sure he was dead. He pissed himself and I let him drop to the floor. I took out my gun and put two in his fucking head." Agent Powell turns to McMahon and shakes his head from side to side.

McMahon asks Primo, "You broke his neck and you knew he was dead, so why did you shoot him?"

"It's my signature, that's how I sign my work." There's silence in the car. After a while McMahon speaks. "Primo, do you know what *modus operandi* means?"

"No."

"It means you're in deep shit cause your signature can tie you to two other murders."

Primo is still staring ahead, and he says "What do you want me to do?"

"You know the phone, the old school payphone on the wall at DiNapoli's Social Club?"

"Yeah, I know it."

"Well, we want you to put a bug in it, and put a few more around the club so we can listen in."

"I can't do that. If Richie finds out I'm a dead man."

"If you don't, you'll have to answer for one—possibly three murders. Take a minute, Primo. Think about it."

"Why are you guys always after Richie?"

"Why?" McMahon responds "Cause he's a killer and a drug dealer. He extorts people, and has people killed if they cross him. You ever kill for him, Primo?"

"I ain't saying nothing about that. But I did overhear something Richie said once at that strip club, Ball Breakers. Something about cutting some drugs, and Dom said it'll still be stronger than most shit on the street."

Agent Powell asks, "Did you overhear where it's coming from or when?"

"No, Richie never tells me anything about his business."

McMahon says, "I'm afraid that's not good enough, Primo. So did you decide?"

Primo looks at McMahon and pauses. Finally he says, "Can I tell you a story?"

"Sure, Primo. Go ahead."

"My mother died a couple of years ago. She made a great sauce, and she always told me to learn how to cook. She used to say 'your mother won't be here forever.' She had a thimble collection from all over the world, and she was very proud of it. She showed her collection to everybody who visited the apartment. I was at her bedside the day she died, and I promised her that I would take care of her collection."

McMahon and the agents look at each other with puzzled expressions. Primo continues, "Once a week I take them out and I clean them. It takes a long time cause there's at least 100 of 'em. If I go to prison there'll be nobody left to do that." The words are not fully out of Primo's mouth when he grabs the seatbelt of Agent Powell, wraps it around his neck and yanks it back, pinning him against the seat. His left hand is wrapped around McMahon's throat. Agent Powell is struggling to get the belt from around his neck. The strength of Primo is overwhelming, and McMahon struggles to reach her gun. Agent Ruiz pulls his gun and aims it at Primo but before he has a chance to shoot, Primo lets go of the seat belt and slams the agent's head against the driver side window, temporarily stunning him. Agent Powell is gasping and coughing, still trying to free himself, as Primo grabs the belt again. McMahon is on the verge of blacking out. She pulls her gun and fires point blank into Primo's gut. The bullet passes through Primo's massive body and shatters the car window behind him. Primo is still holding McMahon by the throat but now his body weight is on top of her. His face is beet red and he's wheezing from his wound. His mouth is filling with blood. He and McMahon lock eyes and McMahon puts the barrel of her gun against Primo's forehead. He mouths the words "Kill me."

Agent Ruiz yells, "No!" He knows what a 9mm bullet will do to a skull at that range. For McMahon, it's now life and death and she fires. Bits of skull, brain and blood splatter the inside of the car and its occupants. Agent Powell shouts "Drive, fucking drive!" The car peels out from the parking lot with tires screeching, followed by the other car. With sirens and lights flashing they reach speeds of 100 miles an hour. Agent Powell shouts, "Get to the safe house!" His voice is dry and raspy. McMahon is leaning against the corner of the back seat, shaking and unable to compose herself. Primo's body is at her feet, and it twitches its last second of life like the whale being torn apart by the sharks. She stares out the window to avoid looking at the bloody mess at her feet. She begins to compose herself and feels pity for Primo and anger at herself for not having more control over the situation. Agent Powell turns and asks McMahon, "Are you alright?" She looks at him and says, "What the fuck do you think?"

A few blocks from the safe house the cars run silent so as not to draw attention. The warehouse gate goes up and the cars drive in. The safe house is an old warehouse garage. It's large, cold and most of it is dirty. There are several desks with computers and large monitors on the wall. The monitors keep vigil on the street around the building. Ebersole comes from behind his desk and walks to the cars. As he gets closer he notices the smashed window and the blood splatters. He walks quickly to the car as McMahon jumps out, covered with gore. The other men exit the car in the same condition. Ebersole looks inside and sees what's left of Primo. He screams, "What the fuck happened?"

Agent Powell says, "Ask Miss Las Vegas here—she fucked it up."

McMahon responds, "You had your back turned—you were supposed to cover him, asshole. Where were you?"

Agent Powell says, "I was getting choked, bitch."

Captain Ebersole shouts, "Everybody shut up, shut the fuck up!" He asks Agent Powell to tell him what happened. Agent Powell replies "We put him in the back seat with McMahon. She told him about the evidence we had. He copped to the murder of Sallie Boy. Told us how he did it in detail—even that Sallie Boy pissed himself before he died."

"Was he gonna cooperate?" Ebersole asks.

McMahon answers, "No."

Ebersole turns to the driver, "And then?"

The driver continues, "He started talking about his mother and her collection."

"Collection, collection of what?"

"Thimbles, Captain."

"Thimbles, a collection of thimbles, who the fuck collects thimbles? Then what happened."

"He went crazy and wrapped the seatbelt around Powell's neck and then he grabbed McMahon by the throat and he was choking her."

Ebersole turns to McMahon. "Is that the way it happened."

"Yeah, he was trying to kill me, so I blew his fucking brains out."

Ebersole asks, "How'd he get his cuffs off?" There's silence. Again he asks, "How'd his cuffs come off? Did you cuff him?" Ebersole gets in Agent Ruiz's face. "Was he cuffed?" Agent Powell responds, "No, he wasn't." Ebersole says it louder. "Was he cuffed?" "No, Captain. He wasn't," answers Agent Ruiz. Ebersole turns to McMahon and asks, "Why wasn't he cuffed, McMahon?"

"Don't know, it wasn't my call."

Ebersole screams angrily, "You're fucking cops—that's the first thing you do, especially with a guy like this. He's a suspect in 3 - count 'em, 3 - murders. You acted like a bunch of rookies. What made you think he wouldn't kill you, assholes? Didn't I tell you to be careful? What the fuck were you thinking?"

The other people in the room are silent. McMahon asks "Where can I get cleaned up." A woman at a keyboard answers, "there's bathrooms upstairs." McMahon says thanks and walks to the stairway. Ebersole turns to the two men and says "Take the car and that fucking mess in the back seat and get rid of it. All of you get the fuck out of here."

Ebersole is sitting at his desk staring into space. McMahon comes down the stairs and sits down at Ebersole's desk. There's silence and the people in the room continue to work.

Ebersole looks at McMahon and says, "This turned to shit quick. Now what, McMahon? He was gonna be the guy to help us put the puzzle together."

"Now we go back to square one. I gotta go." She gets up to leave. Ebersole says, "Primo was gonna die one way or another—it just happened to be you. You're a mess, you can't go outside like that. I'll have one of my agents drive you to your hotel."

"Thanks, Captain."

# CHAPTER 34

# PRIMO'S BODY FOUND

DiNapoli is waiting at his home in Oceanview, Long Island. It's not like Primo to be late. You could usually set your watch to him, but today he's over an hour late. Richie's phone rings. "Yeah, Dom, I know you're waiting. He ain't here yet."

"Did he call you?"

"No, and this ain't like him. Hope he's ok. Is Maxie with you?"

"Yeah we're both waiting." "Hey, Dom. Do me a favor. Go over to Primo's place and see if you can find out what's going on. Maybe he's sick or something. He ain't picking up his phone. Something's up."

"Maybe he did a Mama Cass and choked on a ham sandwich."

"Don't be an asshole, Dom. Go ahead over there, I'll pick up Maxie. We'll meet at the club."

Dom arrives at the Social Club and tells Richie he had no luck at Primo's house. "I looked through the windows, rang the bell, all that shit. Even his car is still there. You don't think the feds grabbed him, do you, Richie?"

"Don't know. But even if they did, he doesn't know shit, and what he knows will implicate him, too."

Dom gets up to leave and Richie asks, "Where the fuck you going? It's early."

"Home. It's my wife's birthday. I told her I would take her to a nice restaurant."

"Hey, Dom. Why don't you take her to Bella's across the street? Tell her to meet you there."

"Sure Richie, that's real classy. See you tomorrow."

Dom is driving the seven miles to his house. He hears breaking news on the Radio. "Primo Delicato, an alleged member of the DiNapoli crime family, was found dead this morning behind an abandoned factory in the Bayshore section of Brooklyn. The victim was shot twice at close range. We'll have more news stories on our 11 pm report."

Dom pulls over and turns off the engine. "Motherfucker," he says to nobody in particular. He calls Richie. Richie answers, "Yeah, Dom, ain't you home yet?"

"Get ready, Richie. I just heard Primo's dead, he was shot twice." There's silence on the other end of the phone. Dom continues, "They found him in Brooklyn behind some old factory."

"Shit, Dom. Sounds like a hit." Richie says to Maxie, "Primo's dead —they found his body in Brooklyn. What the fuck! I can't believe it! We would have heard if he overstepped his bounds and pissed somebody off. If this was sanctioned I wanna know who ordered it."

Maxie says, "Primo was made—if somebody took a contract, it had to be sanctioned."

Richie pauses. "I can't believe Primo's dead. Find out what you can, Maxie."

"I'll call Fuller to see if he knows anything."

"If this wasn't sanctioned, I wanna know so I can return the favor."

"I'll ask around, Richie."

"Thanks, Maxie. I can't believe he's dead."

McMahon is at the airport waiting for her flight back to Las Vegas. She decides to call Rodriguez to let him know about Primo.

Rodriguez answers "Hey, Sarge. How's it going?"

"I'm at JFK."

"No shit! You're in New Yoek? That's great!"

"Yeah, I was, but I'm going back to Vegas."

"Back to Vegas—what do you mean?"

"I got a call a few days ago from Brooklyn organized crime. Remember Captain Ebersole? He's working the case with us. They had new evidence linking Primo to one - possibly three - murders. Ebersole had a plan to pick up Primo and use the evidence to flip. They wanted to bug the phone in the Social Club. They've been trying to bug it for a long time. This was their chance."

"Sounds like a good plan, but I'm getting the feeling something went wrong."

"It's worse than that, Rodriguez. We had Primo in the car and we were talking, just talking when suddenly he went crazy and things went into the shitter real fast. He started choking me, everything was spinning, I couldn't breathe and I was about to pass out, so I put my gun against his forehead and blew his brains out."

There's silence on the other end of the line. After a while McMahon says, "I gotta go—they're calling my flight."

# CHAPTER 35

# SANCHEZ AND DINAPOLI —THE DINNER

Four men are seated at a table in an Italian restaurant owned by a friend of Richie's. Richie is becoming paranoid, especially after Primo's death. He doesn't know who to trust. The people at the table are Richie, Maxie, Dom and Sanchez. Sanchez says, "Mr. Delacruz will have the merchandise available for pickup on Sunday at 11pm. Warehouse number 10 at the Brooklyn Navy Yard. Diego Vargas will be there to handle the transaction. The security guards all have the night off except for the front gate. He'll let you in." Richie looks around the table at the men seated there and he says, "The four of us at this table are the only ones who know about our arrangement with Delacruz."

Dom asks, "What about Fuller?"

"Yeah, about Fuller, my trust for him ran out a long time ago."

"I'll take care of Fuller, I'll figure something out."

"Like I said, nobody knows, only us and Delacruz. Got it, Antonio?"

Richie is staring at Antonio. "Why are you looking at me?"

Richie replies, "'Cause you're a loose cannon with a big mouth. Can I trust you to keep this quiet? Can I, Antonio?"

"Don't worry about me, Richie. When this deal is done I'm gettin' outta Dodge. Pay me and I'm gone, Richie."

Richie is still staring at Antonio and he takes a sip of his wine. "Ok, Antonio. After we get the product, you get paid. Don't fuck with me and things will go smoothly."

Richie picks up the menu and asks who's hungry. Dom says, "I could eat."

After dinner, Richie goes across the street to the Social Club and calls Fuller. Fuller picks up the phone though he's half asleep. "Yeah," he answers.

"Did I wake you, Fuller? Sorry for the late hour. I got some news that's gonna put a smile on your face."

"What's that Richie?"

"What are you doing Sunday night at 11:30?"

"You tell me."

"We're having a party on Pier 86 at my warehouse and you're invited. Make sure to wear something festive."

"Got it, Richie. I'd be happy to attend."

"Good night, Fuller.

# CHAPTER 36

# FULLER, RAT OR NOT

The next morning, Richie and his crew are in the Social Club. Dom and Maxie are talking and laughing loudly—probably on espresso overload. Richie leans over to Dom. "Dom!" Richie calls. Dom keeps talking and laughing loudly. Again Richie calls Dom, but he still doesn't respond. Richie says a little louder, "I got rid of Fuller last night." All of a sudden there's silence. Dom says, "You didn't …" and he makes a pistol gesture with his hands.

Richie says, "I see I finally got your fucking attention. No, he's still alive. What did you hear about Primo? Did you find anything out?"

"No Richie, my contacts don't know shit. If it was sanctioned, nobody's talking. Fuller doesn't know shit, either."

"Speaking of Fuller, how long has he been on our payroll?"

"About five years."

"He's about to be tested. I called him last night and I told him the drop was 11:30 at our pier. Pier 86, where we keep our trucks. Half hour later and 10 miles from the actual drop. Next to our warehouse there's a storage facility—put one of our guys in there. If he sees police activity, we'll know he's a rat. If Fuller is standing there by himself with his dick in his hand, maybe I was wrong about him."

"What if he did turn on us, Richie? He knows our business."

"What does he know? He knows nothing. Let me tell you something about Fuller—he's a pedophile fucking freak—he's got a thing for underage girls. He goes to this joint in Flushing owned by some Asian scumbags."

"How do you know?"

"I did some business with these gook pricks and they owed me a favor. They told me Fuller's a regular there. It was either pay him off or shoot him in the face, and killing a cop is not a good idea."

Dom says. " So Fuller's a pedophile. What do you know? The sick fuck."

"Why don't we just blackmail him, boss?"

"Not a good idea, because when the shit hits the fan, who are they gonna believe? Don't worry about Fuller. Sunday we'll know where he stands."

# CHAPTER 37

# FULLER REVEALED BY MRS. SADIE KLEIN

**R**odriguez is at the precinct talking with the other officers. From across the room an officer shouts, "Rodriguez! You might want to take this on line 2. It's a woman calling about a young girl, could have something to do with your missing person case."

"Hello, Mrs. Cooper."

"Hello, I'm not Mrs. Cooper. My name is Sadie Klein, Mrs. Sadie Klein."

Rodriguez says, "I'm sorry, Mrs. Klein. I thought you were someone else. I'm Detective Rodriguez. What can I do for you?"

"Well, detective, there was quite a ruckus outside my door a few nights ago."

"Ruckus? What kind of ruckus, Mrs. Klein?"

"You see, Detective, I'm a virtual shut-in, and since my Maxwell died—he was my husband—my health is getting worse. I can hardly walk around my apartment."

"I understand, Mrs. Klein. Tell me about the ruckus."

"Well, a few nights ago I was watching my favorite television show. At around 10:30 I hear loud noises from the apartment next door. There was a man talking loudly as if he was angry. Then I heard the door slamming a few times."

"Go ahead, Mrs. Klein."

"I heard sobbing in the hallway and I opened the door just a little, and I was mortified by what I saw, Detective. Standing in the hall was a girl of no more than 17 or 18 years old. All she was wearing were her tops and bottoms."

"What do you mean, Mrs. Klein?"

"Just her underwear, Detective."

"I get it, go ahead."

"Her clothes and some money were strewn all over the floor."

"Are you sure she was in the apartment next door?"

"Oh yes, Detective. You see, there's only four apartments on this floor. She was definitely next door."

"Do you know the person who lives next door?"

"No, I only hear him leave, and sometimes when he comes home. Since I don't get out much, I hardly see anybody."

"May I have your address, Mrs. Klein?"

"Of course, Detective, but I don't need to get involved, do I? You see, I'm 77 years old, and I'd prefer not to be a witness or anything like that."

"I'll make sure of it. Tell me your address, please."

"It's the condominiums on the water. 724 Oakwood Drive. in Oceanview."

"I know the building well, Mrs. Klein. And what is your apartment number?"

"I'm in apartment 3B."

"Ok, Mrs. Klein, apartment 3B. I have your phone number. I'll keep you informed. Is there anything else?"

"Yes, there is. It's a name that she said, but my memory is failing me lately."

"Take your time."

"The girl said the man's name and it started with an F… it's coming to me, I'm playing it over in my head … yes, Detective. She said Fuller."

"Fuller. Are you absolutely sure, Mrs. Klein?"

"Yes, and it's all coming back to me. She said he was a cop and she knew it. But I don't think that's true. A policeman would never treat a young girl like that."

Rodriguez is silent.

"Detective? Are you there, Detective?"

The voice snaps him back. "Thank you, Mrs. Klein. You've been very helpful. I'll be in touch. Good bye, Mrs. Klein."

"Good night, Detective."

# CHAPTER 38

# THE DISCUSSION
# ABOUT FULLER

**M**cMahon is at home a few days after Primo's death. Rodriguez calls her.

"Hi Sarge, how're you doing?"

"I'm ok."

"Listen, Sarge, about the Primo thing —I'm here if you wanna talk."

"Thanks. I appreciate that, Detective, but that's not the reason you called, is it?"

"No, not entirely. I got a call today from a woman who lives next door to Sergeant Fuller. She told me that a few nights ago she heard noises from the apartment. It sounded like people arguing, then she heard the door slamming a few times. She peeked into the hallway, and saw a girl about 17 years old. She was crying and picking up her clothes, and there was money all over the floor."

"And you think it's Fuller's apartment?"

"Yeah, I do. I checked the address and the apartment number, and Fuller lives next door. Right after the door slammed, the woman, her name is Sadie Klein, heard the girl say 'I know you're a cop.' She also said his name was Fuller."

"Shit, Rodriguez, this is nuts. Can Mrs. Klein ID the girl if we found her?"

"I suppose, but she asked me to keep her out of it."

"So what do you want to do, Sarge?"

"There's not much we can do. Our chances of finding the girl are practically zero."

"May I make a suggestion, Sarge? I want to follow him. I think there's more to Fuller than meets the eye."

McMahon answers, "I'm not comfortable with this—after all, he's your boss."

"He's not my boss, Sarge. You are."

"So, Detective, I assume you want my seal of approval to follow him."

Rodriguez answers, "It would be nice, but I'm gonna do it anyway."

There's a pause. "Ok, Rodriguez. Go ahead." McMahon disconnects.

# CHAPTER 39

# FULLER (SHORT EYES)

Fuller leaves the precinct a few hours before his shift ends. He drives west on the Long Island Expressway towards Flushing. He's unaware that he's being followed by a black sedan. He exits at the Main Street exit, and proceeds down dark streets past old buildings and boarded up Asian restaurants, 'for sale' signs are everywhere.

He stops in the middle of a row of apartment buildings that are not as run down as the others in the area. The address is 47-18 Murray Street. The building is one block from Flushing Bay. Rodriguez stops on the corner of the block behind Fuller's car. He watches as Fuller exits his car and walks towards the building.

Rodriguez is following Fuller undetected.

Fuller walks up the front steps to the outside doors. He rings the top bell and he gets buzzed in. Rodriguez watches as Fuller goes in and walks up the steps to the left. He sees the camera over the bell and stays out of its range. He's able to catch the door just before it closes. He goes to the bottom of the stairs and listens for Fuller's footsteps. He ascends the marble steps one floor below Fuller as Fuller reaches the third floor. Rodriguez is just below that floor and slowly moves into position that enables him to see which apartment fuller goes to. He knocks on the door of apartment #2. The knocks are more like a code—there's three knocks with a long pause, then two knocks. The door opens and Fuller enters. He's greeted by name when he enters. It's a woman's voice. Rodriguez waits on the landing above. About one hour later Fuller opens the door to leave and a woman says goodbye to Fuller. She speaks with an Asian accent. Fuller goes downstairs, and the outside door closes behind him. Rodriguez goes down one staircase and approaches apartment #2.

He doesn't have a plan of action. He suspects it's human trafficking, but what he finds inside will shock him. He uses the same code Fuller used and knocks on the door. A voice from inside says, "You forget something?"

"Yeah," Rodriguez answers.

The door opens and a small Asian woman stands in front of him. She's blocking his path, but that doesn't stop him and he pushes past her. He makes believe he's drunk. The Asian woman says, "Get out. I don't know you." He scans the room and sees girls as young as 14, some with bruises on their bodies. He continues his drunk act.

"You don't know me, I don't know you, we don't know anybody— where's Harry? I'm looking for Harry."

The Asian woman tries to push him out, saying, "You go—no Harry here."

Rodriguez replies, "Yeah, he told me to meet him here."

He looks to the back of the apartment and sees a long corridor with 5 rooms on each side. He hears sobbing coming from the back. He begins to walk towards the back when the Asian woman shouts something in a language Rodriguez doesn't understand. From the back of the room two men approach and block his path. "Get out," one of the men says. Rodriguez says, "You're not Harry."

The other man says, "Go, or we throw you down the stairs."

"Ok, Ok. I'm leaving. I don't like Chinese food anyway, it gives me gas."

The Asian woman yells at Rodriguez and the two men make sure he goes down the stairs. Rodriguez turns and says, "If you see Harry tell him I was looking for him. Thanks and good night." He goes down the stairs singing as loud as he could—"Everybody was Kung Fu fighting"—while still acting drunk."

# CHAPTER 40

# MCMAHON LEARNS
# ABOUT THE PEDOPHILE

odriguez calls McMahon. "Two calls in a row, Detective. I'm honored."

"I've got some news about Fuller and it's not good. A few nights ago I followed him to an area of Queens known for teenage prostitutes and runaways. He cruised the area for a while and left."

"Maybe he didn't like the merchandise."

"But tonight I saw Fuller's dark side. He drove to a location in Flushing. There's a building right off Flushing Bay on Murray Street. He entered and went to apartment #2. He was in there for about an hour. When he left I was able to get inside and I saw underage girls, very young girls."

"How did you get inside?"

"It's a long story, Sarge. Let's just say I was not welcome and I was shown the door. I noticed that some of the girls had bruises on their bodies. In the back of the apartment there was a long corridor with private rooms, about 5 or 6 on each side. The witch at the front apparently knew Fuller. She called him by name."

"The witch at the front? What do you mean?"

"There's a camera downstairs before you get inside right above the door bell. The woman at the front desk monitors who rings the bell, and she can see who's coming in. If you stay close to the wall she won't see you."

"What time did Fuller get there?"

"Seven 'o' clock on the dot. He leaves at six 'o' clock a few nights a week."

"Let's suppose Fuller has an appointment with a particular girl at seven 'o' clock once or twice a week—would that make sense?"

"It makes a lot of sense—if it's by appointment, the witch can control who comes and goes."

"When you were inside, you said you were shown the door. By whom?"

"Two big guys threatened to show me out and throw me down the stairs if I didn't leave."

"Is there a back way out, Detective?'

"Yes, there's a fire escape in the back, Sarge."

"Did you see anybody else inside?"

"No, just the two assholes and the woman in the front."

"Are you thinking what I'm thinking, Sarge?"

"Yeah, I am. With Primo gone, Fuller is our only hope of getting DiNapoli."

"But what if he's not on DiNapoli's payroll? This whole thing could blow up in our face."

"I got a feeling about Fuller when I first met him. If we hit the place with him inside we can squeeze him and he'll make a deal. Next time he leaves early—follow him. If he heads to Flushing, we'll be there."

"I'll notify Ebersole and let him know we need his help. I'll catch the next flight out."

# CHAPTER 41

# THE PINCH

Rodriguez is at his desk in the precinct. Fuller pokes his head through the door and says, "I'm out—dentist appointment. See you tomorrow."

"Ok, Sarge. See ya." The clock on his desk says 6 o'clock. He goes down the back stairs to his car parked around the rear of the precinct, and waits in his car until Fuller drives by. He follows him at a safe distance and calls McMahon. "Fullers heading towards Flushing. I'll let you know when he's close."

"He's going to 47-18 Murray St. Approach from 18th Avenue—you can't see it from the apartment. I'll meet you there."

McMahon calls Ebersole. "He's on the move heading towards Flushing. It's 47-18 Murray Street—we'll meet on 18th Avenue."

"I got 6 men leaving now, and we got 4 uniforms on loan from NYPD."

"I'm almost there, see you on 18th Avenue."

Rodriguez calls McMahon: "Fuller is about ten minutes away—what about Ebersole?"

"He's en route," McMahon says.

Rodriguez is the first to arrive; he turns the corner and parks on 18th Avenue. Fuller is inside the apartment. McMahon arrives and walks to Rodriguez's car. "When Ebersole gets here we'll figure out how to get inside."

"Don't worry, Sarge. I'll get us inside."

Ebersole arrives on the scene. McMahon walks over and says, "Thanks, Captain. We appreciate your help on this one. Is he in the apartment, Sergeant?"

"Yeah, he's in there."

"Detective Rodriguez says he can get us inside."

At that moment Rodriguez walks over and addresses Ebersole. "You must be Captain Ebersole. I'm Detective Rodriguez," and he extends his hand. They shake hands, and Rodriguez says, "He's up there, got here about ten minutes ago."

Ebersole asks "Any ideas on how to get in there?"

"Yeah, leave it to me—we're old friends. Where is he?" Ebersole asks.

"He's on the third floor—Apartment #2."

In the background, Ebersole's officers are donning bullet proof vests and checking weapons. Ebersole says, "I understand you've been inside, Detective—what are we up against?"

"Two, probably more, armed and with a bad attitude. There's a woman at the front of the apartment who controls who comes in and out. I like to call her the witch. When you meet her, you'll know why. There's a bell on the outside doors and a camera. Stay close to the wall and the camera won't see you. I'll get us inside."

Ebersole addresses his officers. "There are civilians up there so be surgical, let's not go up there with guns blazing." He turns to McMahon and asks, "What about the girls?"

"Child Protective Services is waiting to take the minors. As for the adults, your guess is as good as mine."

Ebersole addresses his men again: "I want you uniforms to cover the back—there's a fire escape back there if anybody comes down grab 'em. Two of my agents will cover the front, nobody in or out. The rest of you with me. Once inside, McMahon will take over. You good with that, McMahon?"

"Sure. I got it, Captain."

"Ok, Rodriguez. Lead the way."

Rodriguez says, "Stay close to the wall—when they open the door, we move."

Rodriguez has his gun in hand and he climbs the front stairs of the building. McMahon and Ebersole's officers are on either side of Rodriguez. He rings the bell and a voice answers: "What do you want—go away." Rodriguez acts drunk again. "Is Harry there?" There's no reply from the intercom. He rings again and the ring is answered again.

"Go away!"

"Tell Harry I'm here." McMahon and Ebersole look at each other and they're not sure about what's going on.

The woman tells two of her enforcers to "go downstairs and fix it, teach him a lesson." Rodriguez rings the bell again, and the two men open the door. One of the men says, "You asked for it, asshole." Rodriguez lifts his gun and points it in the man's face as Ebersole's officers run inside. Rodriguez tells the men to drop their weapons, and they are cuffed by Ebersole's officers and taken away. McMahon and Rodriguez run upstairs to where Ebersole and his officers are waiting. They hear a woman yelling in a language nobody understands. Ebersole signals one of his men to break down the door. McMahon says, "I got the witch." The officers rush in, and the witch is reaching for something under the desk. McMahon points her gun at her.

"Keep your hands where I can see them." The woman keeps speaking in the same language. McMahon says, "I think we need a translator."

Rodriguez replies, "Don't let her bullshit you. She speaks English."

He goes to the back and empties the rooms. The girls and johns are led to the middle of the apartment. In room number 8 he finds Fuller, and with him is a young girl of no more than 15. Rodriguez takes her robe, hands it to her and motions to her to go outside. He tells Fuller to get dressed and stay in the room. One of Ebersole's agents stays with him." Rodriguez returns to the middle of the apartment. Ebersole's men are in control of the situation, questioning the johns and processing the underage girls. The four NYPD officers come back in with three suspects in handcuffs. One of the officers says, "We found these guys going down the fire escape; they had some serious firepower on them." The officers walk past Rodriguez. One of the suspects glares at Rodriguez, and he's recognized. Rodriguez tells the officer: "Wait a minute, hold up," and he walks over to the suspect, gets in his face and says, "Hey, tough guy, you still wanna throw me down the stairs?"

The suspect says, "Take the cuffs off, cop."

Rodriguez looks at the officer and says, "You got the keys." The officer glances nervously at McMahon and Ebersole.

McMahon says, "Knock it off, Rodriguez. Have your pissing contest some other time."

The suspect says, "Yeah, cop, some other time."

Rodriguez leans in and sings in a low voice: "Everybody was Kung Fu fighting."

McMahon says "Enough, Rodriguez. Get 'em out of here, officers."

## CHAPTER 42

## FULLER FLIPS

Rodriguez and McMahon go into room number eight; the room is barely big enough for a twin bed. A red bulb hanging from the ceiling is the only illumination. By the bed is a nightstand, and on it is a glass bowl full of wrapped condoms. Fuller is staring at the floor while seated on the bed.

McMahon says, "You're under arrest. I'll take your gun and badge."

Fuller says to Rodriguez, "You can't do this to me. I'm your boss..."

Rodriguez replies, "No, you're not. She is."

"I'm Sergeant Elizabeth McMahon with the Las Vegas DEA. I'm gonna skip past the bullshit, Fuller. How old is that girl?"

Fuller responds, "I don't know."

Rodriguez looks at McMahon and says to Fuller: "Just being in the same room with a girl her age can get you five years. Plus all the other shit we're gonna pile on top."

"What's the DEA doing in Flushing, raiding this joint?" Fuller asks.

McMahon says, "We're investigating a shipment of cocaine that's coming from Colombia. An alliance between Delacruz and DiNapoli, and we think you have information that could be helpful to us."

"Me, no way. I don't know anything about it."

Rodriguez says, "We know you're on DiNapoli's payroll."

McMahon looks at Rodriguez with a puzzled expression on her face. Rodriguez continues, "You heard about Primo?"

"Yeah, somebody whacked him."

Rodriguez says, "Yeah, he got whacked, but before that he told us about a deal between DiNapoli and Delacruz, and how you were involved."

"Bullshit! DiNapoli never discussed business with Primo around."

"How would you know that, Fuller?" McMahon asks.

Fuller realizes he said too much. He doesn't say another word and continues to stare at the floor.

Rodriguez asks, "Is Sanchez involved?"

Fuller asks, "You gonna read me my rights?"

Just then there's a knock on the door. It's Ebersole. "We're wrapping it up out here, just letting you know we're out." The door opens and Ebersole goes inside. "Shit, this is a tiny room."

Rodriguez says to Ebersole, "This is Sergeant Bob Fuller from the 18th."

At that point McMahon asks Ebersole, "Can we speak privately, Captain?" They leave the room and go to the outer foyer. "We're gonna need your safe house for a while."

"For what?"

"Fuller's not part of this operation. He's a suspect."

"Continue."

"It seems Sergeant Fuller has short eyes. We also think he's on DiNapoli's payroll. With Primo gone, he's our last chance. We wanna take him to the safe house so we can interview him further."

"What do you expect to get out of him?"

"We wanna find out about this shipment from the Delacruz cartel. We wanna know where and when."

"Did he ask for a lawyer yet? If he does, this whole thing falls apart."

"Then we gotta make sure he doesn't."

Rodriguez comes out of the room with Fuller, who says, "I'm not saying another word without a lawyer."

McMahon asks, "Do you really want a lawyer involved? If you lawyer up, it all comes out—the underage girls, cruising for hookers, that girl you assaulted and threw out of your apartment. How old was she, Fuller? Your involvement with DiNapoli, it's going to be out there for all to see. It's your choice. Help us out and we'll see about returning the favor. Lawyer up, and there's no deal."

Fuller thinks for a minute and says, "Ok, I wanna deal. Now what?"

"Now we go with Captain Ebersole to a house in Brooklyn where you'll be under, shall we say, house arrest. If any information you give us is good, we'll talk about a deal."

Captain Ebersole adds, "We're ready to roll."

McMahon says, "Cuff him."

"You think that's necessary, Sarge? He's unarmed and he ain't going anywhere."

"I said put the cuffs on him."

"Ok. Sorry, Fuller, but you heard the lady."

Rodriguez cuffs Fuller and asks McMahon, "Can we at least go down the backstairs?"

"Sure, as long as he's cuffed." They go downstairs and climb into three cars. Ebersole says to McMahon, "Fuller is gonna ride with me." McMahon and Rodriguez are riding together and there's silence in the car. Finally Rodriguez asks McMahon, "Why did you insist I cuff him? He didn't have any weapons, and after all, he's a cop. I didn't want to humiliate him in front of the other officers."

"When we picked up Primo we didn't cuff him, and we were talking to him in the car. He was calm, he didn't say much. We confronted him with the evidence against him, and he admitted he killed Sallie Boy. We told him we wanted information on DiNapoli. He refused to help us and then he started talking about his mother. He went crazy and wrapped that big fucking hand of his around my neck like he did Sallie Boy. I pulled my weapon and fired one round into his gut—nothing, no reaction. I put the next round between his eyes. It was murder by cop. And that's how Primo died. Now you know why I wanted him cuffed."

"And what was that shit about Primo telling us that Fuller was involved with DiNapoli and Delacruz?"

"It worked, didn't it, Sarge?"

"Yeah, I guess whatever works."

# CHAPTER 43

# PLANNING TOM'S DEMISE

Sanchez and Felix are playing pool at Ball Breakers. Sanchez finishes his game and tells Felix, "Let's go to the room. I gotta talk to you. It's time to pay your debt to me."

"What are you talking about, Antonio?"

"Not here. Let's go to the office."

The men enter the backroom and close the door behind them. Antonio opens the fridge and offers Felix a beer. Felix declines, but Antonio opens one and takes a big swallow. He says, "Sunday night we're gonna do the war hero."

Felix asks, "Why Sunday?"

"Cause Sunday I get paid after I do this deal."

"This guy didn't do nothing to me. I don't want to kill him."

"Listen Felix, you owe me. I helped you get rid of the body, and you didn't get caught. Without me you'd be in jail right now—just another sad sack inmate looking at serous time."

"I can't do this, man."

"Yes, you can and will. I'm gonna give you a gun and you're gonna shoot the war hero." Antonio's plan is to have Felix shoot Tom. When Tom is dead, Antonio kills Felix. No witnesses, no evidence —Antonio gets his money and leaves the country.

"Here's the plan, Felix. Sunday night we drive to the house and park a block away. I'll go upstairs and get him to open the door. When he does, you shoot him."

"What if he ain't home?"

"Don't matter to me—if he's home, he dies. If he ain't, I got the keys. We go in and we wait. Live or die don't mean a fucking thing to me 'cause either way I'm leaving town. We wait. If he don't show, I'll go take care of my business."

"What about Anna?"

"I'm done with Anna—the bitch played me. Killing the war hero will be punishment enough, knowing she caused this shit."

"What if she's home?"

"She won't be home. She has a class that she never misses. After class they all go out for tea or whatever the fuck. Sunday night I'll pick you up at eight—that's when I'll give you the gun. We drive to the house, we do him, and I'll drive you back to the club—that's your alibi. They'll think you were there all night."

"What about you, Antonio?"

"I got business to take care of."

"What about me, Antonio? We've been friends a long time."

"All good things must end, Felix," Antonio says sarcastically. "I'm gone after Sunday."

# CHAPTER 44

## AT THE SAFE HOUSE

The car arrives at the safe house. In the lead car is Ebersole, Fuller and two of Ebersole's men. Ebersole steps out of the car and tells McMahon, "Let's go upstairs. We can talk to him there." They all go upstairs into a room with a desk and four chairs. In front of the desk is a camera on a tripod. Fuller is still handcuffed, and he sees the camera. He says, "I'm not saying a word till you turn the camera off and take off these fucking cuffs."

McMahon says the camera and the cuffs stay put." "You gotta buy those privileges, Fuller. Give us information and you get something back."

Rodriguez whispers to McMahon, "I wanna take his cuffs off."

McMahon says "No, not yet."

"Trust me—take his cuffs off. I'll have him eating out of my hand."

"No Rodriguez, not yet."

"Can I at least talk to him?

"Sure. Go ahead and talk." Rodriguez walks over to Fuller and whispers, " Listen to me, Fuller I wanna take your cuffs off but my boss won't let me. If I take them off, will you do anything stupid?"

"No, I won't fuck around. Take 'em off."

Rodriguez looks back at McMahon, and she shakes her head no. McMahon tells Ebersole, "Captain, would you ask your agents to excuse us, please?"

Rodriguez says, "It seems I might be the only friend you've got in this building. Sergeant McMahon says they stay on. Sorry, Fuller, I tried."

Fuller says, "I get it, a bad cop, good cop routine, is that what this is? Ain't gonna work with me, I've been a cop too long."

"Let me tell you what this is, Fuller. If I get the feeling that you're not being honest with us or you're fucking with me, I'll throw you around this room, cuffs or no cuffs."

McMahon says, "Easy, Rodriguez. Rodriguez continues, "I don't care what you did for DiNapoli in the past, Fuller, but we're trying to stop a shipment of cocaine, actually cocaine on steroids, from hitting the streets. People who use this shit could die. Tell us when and where, Fuller."

Fuller says, "If I tell you and they find out it was me, I'm a dead man, just like Primo." McMahon and Rodriguez glance at each other. Ebersole says, "Let me tell you something—when you get to prison, you're gonna be a dead man, anyway. You got short eyes and you're a cop. So the way I see it, you've got a better shot with us. Tell us what you know and we'll protect you."

Fuller hesitates for a moment and then he asks, "Is that camera on? If it is, I want it shut off and moved away from me or I'm not saying shit."

Ebersole shuts it off and turns it to the wall. "You happy now, Fuller."

Rodriguez says, "Now tell us about the shipment."

Fuller says, "This Sunday, Pier 86 at 11:30 pm. That's where DiNapoli keeps his trucks. It's at his warehouse."

McMahon asks, "Who else is involved?" Fuller is silent.

Rodriguez says, "Antonio Sanchez. Ain't that right, Fuller?" Fuller nods yes. "How is the merchandise being transported?"

Fuller responds, "I don't know—all I know is the drop is at Pier 86."

McMahon asks, "Who told you?"

"The man himself."

Rodriguez says, "Shit, that only gives us a day and a half."

Ebersole says, "Let me know how I can help. This is your parade, Sergeant."

"Thanks, Captain."

Fuller asks, "What happens now?"

Ebersole answers, "Now you're gonna be our guest for a while."

McMahon and Rodriguez leave the room. McMahon asks, "Do you think the information is good?"

"If it's not, he's fucked. Good night," and he walks down the hall.

McMahon yells, "Where the hell are you going?"

"I'm tired, and I don't feel like driving back to Long Island. I'm looking for a place to sleep in this dump."

# CHAPTER 45

## SADDLE UP

DiNapoli and his men are preparing for the exchange at the Brooklyn Navy Yard. They're in an empty warehouse in Long Island City. The warehouse is owned by RDN Importing, one of DiNapoli's many shell companies. The cocaine will be tested, cut to the desired potency, and distributed from this warehouse.

The men prepare their weapons and DiNapoli tells them, "When we get to the Navy Yard, fan out. Keep your eyes open. Don't be too anxious. The last thing we need is a fucking war."

Dom says to DiNapoli, "What about Sanchez? Richie, what do you want me to do?"

"Leave him alone, Dom. If Delacruz wants him dead, let his guys do it."

"I don't want to get on Delacruz's bad side in case Sanchez is his golden boy."

"When we have the product, I'll keep my word and pay him. But if he fucks us, he's yours, Dom. Maxie, let's roll."

Maxie yells, "Saddle up, fellas. Let's go."

## CHAPTER 46

# SUNDAY NIGHT MASSACRE —TOM IS THE TARGET

Sanchez is on his way to pick up Felix when he arrives at Felix's building. Felix is waiting downstairs, and he enters the car.

"Here, Felix." Antonio hands Felix the gun. "It's loaded. Safety's off —just aim and pull the trigger. Wait till he's close—you can't miss."

"I can't kill nobody. The stripper was an accident—we were both fucked up."

"Yeah, you were both fucked up, but she's dead and you're alive. Now man up, you pussy. You're gonna kill the war hero."

Felix is quiet the rest of the way. They arrive at Tom's house and the lights are out. Sanchez says, "Wait here I'll get the keys." Antonio goes into his house and comes out with the keys to Tom's apartment upstairs. "Come on, Felix, let's go up."

"He ain't home, let's go."

"No, we're gonna wait awhile. If he don't show, he gets to live. It's his lucky night."

The men climb the stairs and Antonio says, "We're gonna wait a while, but not too long, there's some place I gotta be. When he comes in, start shooting and keep shooting till he's dead."

"Antonio I'm shaking. I ain't never shot nobody. I hope he don't come home."

"Hide behind the couch. I'll be in the kitchen." A few minutes later headlights skim the inside of the house. "You better shoot him, Felix, or I'm gonna shoot you."

Tom climbs the stairs and is about to enter the apartment. Felix panics and fires a shot through the door. The bullet strikes Tom in the shoulder. Tom fights through the pain and pushes the door in. Felix continues to shoot wildly as Tom moves about in the dark apartment, deliberately drawing fire. Felix runs out of bullets and screams for Antonio. Felix attacks Tom, trying to pistol whip him. Felix is no match for Tom's 6'3" 200 pound frame. Tom is strong from his days in the military and workouts in the police gym, but Tom is taken by surprise by the strength of Felix, probably drug fueled, who is determined to kill him. The gun comes down on Tom's head and stuns him. Tom's right side is blood soaked from the bullet wound in his shoulder. Tom regains focus, and the two men wrestle for the gun in Felix's hand. Tom wins the battle, and takes the gun from Felix. The gun crashes down on Felix's nose, opening up a deep gash that immediately gushes blood. This shocks Felix, and he again yells for Antonio. He feels the impact of the second blow to the side of the head. Felix punches at Tom's wound, causing pain, but this seems to energize Tom. The gun in Tom's hand comes crashing down on Felix's head again. The feeling of being airborne overtakes Felix, and he wonders if it's because he's going into shock or because of the blows to the head. Felix is lapsing into semi-consciousness as he is thrown through the front window. The last thing he sees is the jagged piece of stained glass protruding from his chest. Felix dies on the porch below. Tom hears

Antonio moving around the kitchen and takes cover behind the couch. "You're a dead man, war hero. I know about you and my wife, and now you're gonna die." Tom moves about to draw fire in the dark. Antonio fires and misses. Tom pulls the gun from his ankle holster. Again he makes noise to draw fire and again Antonio misses. Tom aims at the muzzle flash and fires. Antonio is hit by the bullet grazing him just above his hip. "Motherfucker, you got me! I'm gonna kill you slow, war hero." Antonio fires again and again till he's out of bullets. Tom fires and misses. "You missed, war hero I'm gonna cut you into little pieces, you fucking cabron." Tom moves toward the kitchen, and as he turns he sees Antonio lunging at him with a knife. Tom deflects the attack and punches Antonio in the face. Antonio swings the knife and again it's deflected. Antonio tries to punch Tom in his wound but Tom blocks the punch again and backs up to avoid another lunge of the knife.

Tom reverts to his martial arts background and kicks Antonio in the chest. The speed and the power behind the kick stuns Antonio. Antonio charges Tom with the knife over his head. The knife misses as Tom sidesteps the attack. Antonio punches Tom directly on his wound and Tom reels from the pain. Antonio lunges again and Tom is able to disarm Antonio with a kick to Antonio's wrist. The knife slides across the floor. Antonio feels vulnerable, and he throws his full body weight at Tom. They both fall to the floor with Tom on the bottom. Antonio is flailing punches which Tom is able to deflect. Tom delivers a punch to Antonio's throat causing Antonio to gasp for air and lose focus, which allows Tom to get to his feet. Antonio is attempting to stand, but Tom kicks him in the face. In desperation, Antonio grabs a lamp with a marble base and hits Tom in the knee. Tom falls to the ground and reaches for the knife. Both men struggle for the knife but neither one is successful. Antonio grabs the lamp and swings it towards Tom's head. He strikes a glancing blow and Tom is stunned, but attacks as the lamp crashes against the wall. Blood covers the men and the furniture.

Tom hits Antonio with the lamp and he falls to his knees. Tom wraps the wire around his neck and as Antonio struggles Tom tightens the wire. Antonio's arms are flailing trying to punch Tom from an impossible position. Tom puts his knee in Antonio's back for leverage. Blood and saliva pour out of his mouth. Antonio continues to struggle, but Tom is determined to end it here. Antonio's face is a grotesque death mask with bulging eyes and lips slightly blue.

Tom continues to keep pressure on the wire. He knows Antonio's dead but hatred and adrenaline fuel his strength. Finally, he relinquishes his grip and falls to his side. The room goes dark and unconsciousness overtakes him.

# CHAPTER 47

# INTRODUCING DIEGO

Three large black cars drive through Brooklyn. They're on their way to the Brooklyn Navy Yard to meet the shipment and close the deal. Not far behind is a carting truck belonging to the DiNapoli carting company. They drive through the main gate, and the guard gives them a knowing nod. The group arrives at warehouse #10. The trucks stop in front of the warehouse, and the cars form a semicircle. In the lead car is Richie, Dom and Maxie. They wait till the men in the other two cars exit, carrying semi-automatic weapons. The men fan out, covering the area near the warehouse. When the men are in position, Richie, Dom and Maxie exit the car. From the other end of the pier two cars approach, their headlights lighting up the warehouse and the men waiting there. In the headlights there is a silhouette of three figures, and they approach DiNapoli and his men. When they get close, the man in the middle waves his hand and the night is dark again as the headlights go out. The men are now face to face. The man in charge is Diego; he looks more like a Hugo boss model than a Cartel business manager. With him is Miguel, Delacruz's enforcer and the third man who is very large. Dom leans over to Richie and says, "Don't that guy remind you of somebody?"

Richie replies, "Yeah, Primo must be his twin."

Diego is the first to speak. "Gentlemen, I'm Diego Vargas." He extends his hand to the man in the center, assuming he's the man in charge.

Richie takes his hand and says, "I'm Richie DiNapoli. This is my Lieutenant, Dom, and Maxie, my Counsellor."

Diego now makes his introductions. "This is Miguel. He is, as you would say, Mr. Delacruz's Lieutenant, and this large gentleman is Carlos, but we call him Gordo Carajo."

Richie asks, "what does that mean, what you just said?"

"Fat fuck."

"Don't that bother him, that you call him that?"

"No, you see he's a little slow." He points to his head and lets out a laugh. "Because of it his adversaries underestimate him. But he can snap your neck just like that," and he snaps his fingers in the air for effect.

Maxie says to Richie, "Yeah, just like Primo."

"As for me, my job is simple. I'm Mr. Delacruz's business manager. I put together deals just like this one, and I am paid quite handsomely. So now down to business. Mr. Delacruz wants you to know he thanks you for your trust in him and looks forward to working together."

"Yeah, sure. Me, too."

Richie looks up and down the dock, and all he sees is a crane at the end of the dock. He looks at Diego and asks, "Where's the boat."

Diego looks at Richie as if he doesn't understand. Richie asks again: "The boat with the merchandise—where is it?"

Diego says, "The boat" as he laughs, and his men laugh with him.

DiNapoli's men lift their weapons as do Delacruz's men, anticipating trouble.

Diego says, "There is no boat."

Richie replies, "What the fuck is going on?"

Diego says, "Relax gentlemen. Please, no weapons," and he gestures to his men to lower theirs. "Tranquilo, muchachos. Your merchandise has been here for several days, safe as a baby in its mothers arms. Gentlemen, please observe the crane at the end of the dock." He gestures to the crane's operator and shouts, "Bring it up!" The crane is old and worn, with faded yellow paint and rusted metal. All eyes are on it as it starts up. It makes a roaring sound and black smoke billows from its stack. Richie looks around nervously. Out of a container in the floor of the dock comes a pallet with five crates on it. Maxie says, "Holy shit, look at that."

Diego hears him and explains: "A few years ago Mr. Delacruz purchased some warehouses along these docks. Some were foreclosed, and others were put up for sale by their owners. Those in ground storage units were used to store grain, a long time ago, of course. When shipping moved to containers, that form of storage became obsolete. We converted them to humidity and temperature controlled rooms. That 'free sample' Sanchez gave you to test came from there." He points to the palette. "The Merchandise is the same throughout."

Richie says, "Did you say that was a free sample?"

"Yes, an investment towards future business."

"That fucking Sanchez charged me for that sample."

"He made you pay? How much?"

"Fifty grand, that motherfucker."

"That's typical of that puto. Speaking of Sanchez, where is he?"

"I don't know, he was supposed to be here. All the more reason to get the fuck out of here."

"Too bad Sanchez isn't here. Mr. Delacruz wanted me to give him a present," Dom says, "Colombian necktie."

Diego smiles. "Yes, something like that. Richie says, "Let's load up and move out."

Richie gives the signal, and the back of the truck opens up and the men move the crates into the back of the truck. The truck closes again like the mouth of a giant creature. Diego motions and the warehouse gates go up.

"Mr. Delacruz gives you the use of his warehouse; it has all the comforts of home. I'll be in New York until you test the product and are assured it's as advertised. In the future we'll do business with tons—not kilos—of product."

Diego hands Richie a card and says, "I can be reached at that number."

Richie reads the card—it says "Vargas International Shipping, Diego Vargas, President."

Diego says, "It's bullshit. Call me when you're ready to move the merchandise." He turns and begins walking to a waiting limousine. He turns to Richie and says, "I'll let you buy me dinner at the best restaurant in New York. Italian, of course. Good night, gentlemen."

Richie shouts, "Hey Diego, how did you get the merchandise to New York?"

Diego turns and responds, "By boat, of course." He laughs as he gets into a limousine and it drives away followed by his men.

Richie says to Dom, "Bring the truck inside and stay with the merchandise tonight. Take a few men with you. We'll move it in a few days to Long Island City."

"Why me, Richie? I don't wanna spend the night in some shitty warehouse."

"Dom, who else can I trust? There could be one hundred million bucks of street value in that truck."

"Ok, Richie, I get it. I'll stay tonight."

"Thanks, Dom. I'll get Maxie to stay tomorrow. Tell the men to stay alert, we can't trust anybody. I appreciate it, Dom."

Richie and the remaining men leave the Navy Yard. Minutes later Richie's phone rings. It's Dom.

"Yeah, Dom?"

"Holy shit, Richie, you gotta see this place. It's hooked up like a Park Avenue pad. It's got a full kitchen, champagne in the fridge, cable tv, designer bathrooms, unfuckingbelievable."

Richie laughs and tells Dom, "See Dom, like Diego said—all the comforts of home. I'll ask Maxie about tomorrow night. Ok, Dom?"

"No, that's ok ,Richie. I'll do it tomorrow night, too."

"That's what I thought. Good night, Dom."

Ebersole and McMahon are looking at a map of Pier 86, planning the raid on DiNapoli's warehouse. Ebersole speaks to his people. "Gather round, we're almost ready to go. To my right is Sergeant McMahon, she's on loan from the Las Vegas DEA, with Special Agent Rodriguez. The Sergeant will be second in command on this operation. She knows the drill. She's done this more than once. On the table is a map of Pier 86. Agent Ruiz, take 3 agents and cover the rear of the building here and here. Agent Harris, you take 6 and cover the front. Nobody gets in, nobody gets out. We're gonna run silent and put our cars up here on the street. If you see any security on the pier, flash your badge and bring them up to the cars or tell them to duck and cover. Last thing we want is a bunch of civilians getting hurt. Remember to meet force with force. There's a swat team standing by if we need 'em. Get your vests on and check your weapons."

Ebersole walks over to Sergeant Fuller and says, "You can get comfortable in my office, Sergeant. A couple of my men are gonna stay with you. I'll tell 'em to keep the cuffs off. I'm trusting you to do as they say and don't do anything stupid, otherwise they're gonna cuff you to a chair. This is a courtesy, Fuller. Don't fuck it up."

Fuller says, "if DiNapoli doesn't see me there, he's not making the deal."

"Bullshit, Fuller! It's too late for DiNapoli to turn back now—this ain't a social call. When we hit the pier, the last thing on DiNapoli's mind is gonna be you."

Ebersole motions to his men and they walk over. Ebersole says "I told Fuller as long as he behaves you'll keep the cuffs off, but if he fucks around, handcuff, him to the chair in my office. Don't let him out of your sight."

Ebersole yells to his men, "Let's go, it's an hour to Pier 86."

Two cars and a van leave the safe house, leaving Fuller and three agents behind.

# CHAPTER 49

# THE ESCAPE

Fuller is sitting at one of the desks in the safe house, and one of the agents assigned to watch him says, "Let's go to Ebersole's office. There's a cot in there you may want to grab some sleep."

"Nah, I don't want to sleep. You think there's a gun in one of those drawers?"

"Ebersole says I should cuff you to the chair if you get stupid, so watch your mouth."

"Sure, no problem." Fuller sits behind Ebersole's desk and the agent sits across from him.

"So Fuller, how long have you been a cop?"

"About 30 years."

"And now you fucked it all up."

"I'll be alright. What about you? What's your story, Agent?"

"I've been with Ebersole 8 years, been a cop for 21."

"You wanna play cards? You got cards around here?"

"Nah, I don't play cards with pedophiles."

"Too bad, I'm fucking bored to tears."

"Matter of fact, I'm gonna leave and send someone else in to watch you. I don't like the air in here." The agent leaves. While he's gone, Fuller tries opening the drawers in Ebersole's desk but they're all locked. A young agent comes into Ebersole's office and sits across from Fuller.

Fuller says, "Hi, Rookie. You must be the A-Team. How long have you been with Ebersole?"

The young agent answers, "18 months."

"Shit, 18 months—I got condoms older than you. You are a fucking Rookie. You got a deck of cards, Rookie?"

"No I don't, and don't call me Rookie any more."

An agent from the other side of the room yells, "Hey, Fuller, leave the kid alone or I'll cuff you to the fucking chair."

"Yeah, sure. You got a girlfriend, Rookie?"

"Stop calling me rookie."

"Sorry, so you got a girl?"

"Yeah, I do."

"Is she young?"

"She's my age."

Fuller says "I like 'em young, too. Real young." The other agent yells, "Last warning—one more and you get cuffed to the chair, you fucking freak."

Fuller gets closer to the young agent and says, "Your girlfriend got a younger sister?"

The young agent says, "Fuck you!"

The other agent says, "I'm cuffing you to the chair and if you don't shut up I'm gonna shove a gag in your mouth."

Fuller yells, "I gotta pee!"

The other agent walks over and tells the young agent, "I'll take him upstairs. Come on, Fuller. Let's go. You got five minutes." They go upstairs and the agent waits outside the bathroom door.

Fuller is in the bathroom looking for a weapon. He reaches under the sink and unscrews a pipe about 18 inches long, puts it behind his back and into his waistband. He flushes the toilet, grabs some paper towels and makes believe he's drying his hands. He steps out of the bathroom, puts his hands in the air and tells the agent, "You wanna search me?"

"Put your hands down, let's go back downstairs."

The agent turns his back to go downstairs. Fuller takes the pipe from his waistband and hits the agent. The agent tries to yell for help, Fuller covers his mouth and hits him two more times. The agent is unconscious, and Fuller takes his gun. He drags him into the bathroom and closes the door. Fuller goes out the back and down the stairs. He goes to the garage and is approached by an officer. "Can I help you?"

Fuller says, "Yeah, I'm Sergeant Fuller. I need a car. I'm meeting up with Ebersole—he's on assignment."

"Ok, let me check the list." The officer checks the clipboard for Fuller's name." Sorry, Sergeant. I don't see your name. Ebersole has to approve the cars going out. Do you have an ID?" Fuller reaches into the inside pocket of his jacket and produces the gun. He pistol whips the officer until he's unconscious, grabs a set of keys from a locker and drives away.

# CHAPTER 50

# BAD INFORMATION

Ebersole and the team arrive at pier 86. They park the cars on the street overlooking the pier. From inside the cars they look for activity but it's quiet. McMahon radios to Ebersole. "We need to get a look inside the warehouse."

"You trust Fuller's information, Captain?"

"His ass is on the line—I think he knows better than to fuck with us."

"I hope you're right, Captain. I see an open window—I'll see if I can get inside."

"Careful, Rodriguez." McMahon radios Ebersole. "Rodriguez is gonna try to get inside." Ebersole radios the swat team and his men. "Stand down—one of ours is gonna try and get inside. We move on my signal. Just wait for instructions." Rodriguez crawls through the open window and the back room stinks of garbage. He sees men milling about and trucks with their engines on. The gate to the warehouse goes up and several trucks are lined up to leave.

Rodriguez shouts into his radio "Move in" lights and sirens pierce the quiet on Pier 86. The team moves in and shouts of "Don't move" and "Let me see your hands" echo through the warehouse.

Ebersole walks into the warehouse with gun drawn. The men who were milling about are now lined up with their hands behind their heads. They're not sure what's going on and glance nervously at each other. Ebersole barks: "Who the fuck is in charge here?"

A voice in the line replies, "I am, sir."

Ebersole barks again: "Get over here and keep your hands where they are. What's your name?"

"My name is Joe Delgado and I'm the night manager."

"What's going on, Mr. Manager? And don't bullshit me."

"I don't understand."

"Where's DiNapoli? Is he here?"

"No sir. He never comes here.

Ebersole turns to his men. "Don't stand around—search this fucking place." He asks, " Are these trucks coming or going?"

The manager answers "They're empty. They're going to the city to pick up garbage. They were leaving when you guys got here."

Ebersole pauses and walks up and down. He puts his gun down to his side and turns to McMahon. "Any ideas, Sergeant?"

McMahon replies, "Search the trucks."

Ebersole tells the manager to open a particular truck. The manager steps to the front of the truck and signals the driver to open the back. Even though the truck is empty, the smell is overpowering as the back opens. Ebersole tells two of his men to check it. "But Captain, it stinks!"

Ebersole shouts: "Check the fucking trucks."

The men search the truck and yell back that it's empty.

"Search 'em all, I don't give a fuck if it takes all night."

Captain Ebersole calls over an NYPD officer. "Check these guys for priors. If they got open warrants, hold 'em. The rest can get the fuck out of here. I'm gonna have a look around."

Ebersole's radio squeaks: "Fuller's gone and two of your agents are in bad shape."

Rodriguez says, "I got this. I know where he's going. He's gonna fly his way out of here. He's got a friend—Tom Hartford—who's a pilot. I'll contact you when I find him." Rodriguez takes one of the cars and speeds away.

Ebersole says to McMahon: "Well this was a fucking disaster, McMahon. That's two for two—what's next?"

McMahon responds, "You were there when we questioned him, and your men let him get away. I'm out of here. His information was bullshit; there's nothing here." McMahon contacts Rodriguez and asks, "Detective, where are you?"

"I'm on my way to Sanchez's place. I can't explain now, but it's a house on Meadow Lane that belongs to Sanchez's wife. Give me a head start, then call for backup.

Fuller arrives at Tom's house and runs from his car. He stops when he sees Felix on the porch. He draws his gun and goes upstairs. He looks through the window and sees silhouettes of the men on the floor. Cautiously he enters the apartment and turns on the light. He's shocked by what he sees, blood is splattered everywhere. Sanchez is lying on his side, his face blue and distorted. Tom is unconscious and Bob feels for a pulse. Tom is alive and Fuller calls his name. "Tom, Tom can you hear me? It's Bob." He shakes him a few times, still calling his name. Bob goes to the kitchen and grabs a towel and places it on Tom's wound. He applies pressure and Tom winces. Tom begins to regain consciousness and the room slowly comes into focus. He looks at Fuller and says, "Bob, Sanchez tried to kill me."

"Looks like you got him first. Who's that asshole on the porch?"

"I don't know, he was with Sanchez. He's the one that shot me."

"I think that's Felix; he's one of Sanchez's lackies. Tom, I need your help—you've got to get me out of the country. If you don't, one way or another, I'm a dead man."

"What're you talking about?"

"I'm a dirty cop, Tom. I got involved with DiNapoli years ago and I'm on his payroll. I need you to fly me out of here."

"I can't fly Bob, look at me! I couldn't fly even if I wanted to."

"I got a lot of money stashed away, Tom, there's enough for both of us. We can live like kings, just help me get out. I can fly the plane—just talk me through it."

"I can't Bob, I'll be breaking the law."

Bob aims his gun at Tom and says, "Don't make me shoot you, Tom. I don't want to hurt you."

Just then, head lights light up the windows and Fuller goes to see who it is. He sees Rodriguez coming out of the car with his gun drawn. "It's fucking Rodriguez—how did he know I'd come here."

"You told him I flew a plane, remember."

"Shit, don't make a sound or I'll kill you both." Fuller turns off the light. Rodriguez is walking up the first set of stairs. He sees Felix's body on the porch, he wonders to himself what the fuck is he doing here. If Felix is here, Sanchez is also lurking close by. He rethinks going up the front steps and instead goes to the back of the house. Fuller is tired of waiting and he slowly peeks out the front window looking for Rodriguez. Tom tries to reach for the knife dropped by Sanchez but his attempt is thwarted by Fuller who hits him with the gun on the side of the head. "Try it again and I'll kill you. Now shut the fuck up and I won't hurt you again." Rodriguez is making his way up the back stairs and Fuller turns to face the back door. Rodriguez shouts "Come out, Fuller. Give it up."

Fuller responds, "Come get me, motherfucker."

Rodriguez sees the outline of Fuller and he moves across the door to draw his fire. Fuller fires two rounds and misses. Rodriguez returns fire and also misses the bullet crashing through the window. Fuller fires again and misses, the bullet whizzes past Rodriguez. Tom is regaining his senses and he is able to reach the knife dropped by Sanchez. He stabs Fuller in the leg causing him to fall to one knee. Fuller screams in pain and he turns his gun towards Tom. Rodriguez takes advantage of the distraction and aims towards the noise. As Fuller turns his gun Rodriguez fires twice, hitting Fuller and he falls to the floor mortally wounded. Rodriguez runs over to Tom to see if he could treat his wounds till the ambulance arrives. He stops at Fuller and feels for a pulse. He says to Tom, "Hang in there—help is on the way."

"What about Bob? Is he ..."

Rodriguez interrupts. "Yeah Tom, he's dead. He left me no choice." In the background the sound of sirens and lights penetrate the sky.

---

Richie and Maxie are at the social club the morning after the delivery at the Brooklyn Navy Yard. The pay phone on the wall rings and it's Dom. Maxie picks it up. "Hey Maxie, put on Channel 4 news. Hurry up." Maxie yells across to the waiter, "Put on Channel 4 - quick." On the news there's a special bulletin about the shooting and the three deaths at Tom's house. Richie and Maxie just stare at the TV, not believing what they're hearing. After the bulletin, Richie is still staring at the screen; after a while he goes to the phone. He says to Dom, "See, Dom, like I always told you, there is a God. They're all dead, and last night died with them. Wednesday morning we move the truck to Long Island City. Let Diego know."

"Do you want Maxie to relieve you tonight, Dom?"

"No, Richie. You kidding? I like it here."

'Yeah, that's what I thought."

## CHAPTER 51

## 82

Rodriguez is sitting in his office at the precinct. He's typing reports about the events of Sunday night. The phones at the precinct are ringing off the hook with reporters, and photographers and television stations are outside the precinct hoping for an interview with Rodriguez. McMahon walks into the office, carrying her luggage for the trip back to Las Vegas. "Damn, Rodriguez, you're a popular guy!"

"I could live without it. Are you off to Vegas, Sarge?"

"Yeah, I've got a flight out of JFK. I've had enough of the Big Apple."

"I wanna thank you for your efforts on this one. I know leaving Vegas wasn't easy for you."

"Oceanview wasn't so bad. I got used to it. The peace and quiet, you know what I mean."

"Peace and quiet, my ass—six dead plus a girl you think was killed by Sanchez, a pedophile police sergeant, and a missing drug shipment. Some peace and quiet."

How're you going to the airport, Sarge?"

"I don't know. I guess I'll take a cab."

"I'll give you a ride. I gotta get out of here for awhile."

"That's okay, Detective, I see you're busy."

"I insist, Sarge. We can chat, give us a chance to bond."

"Cut the crap and give me the keys."

"Why?"

"Cause I've seen you drive, Rodriguez, and the idea is to get to the airport before the plane leaves the ground."

"Very funny, Sarge. Okay, let's go." Rodriguez yells to his officers, "I'm heading to the airport. Come on, Sarge, let's go down the back."

Half an hour later they're stuck in traffic. "Well, Sarge, here we are. Any suggestions?"

"Don't worry. I have a lot of time left, I'll make it. So tell me, Detective, what are your plans? Are you thinking about staying in Oceanview? Think when the dust settles you'll get Fuller's spot?"

"I'm not sure. I think I'd miss Vegas. So tell me,Sarge, who else did you have on this?"

"I guess I can tell you now. I had an agent in Ball Breakers posing as a stripper."

"No shit, Sarge!"

"Yeah, I brought her up from Virginia. She went by the name of Cinnamon."

"We've met, Sarge. She helped me the night I got beat up outside the joint."

"Well, well, it's a small world. Take a few weeks, detective, and make your decision. There's a place for you in my Command."

"Thanks, Sarge. So tell me about Cinnamon. How did that work out?"

"It worked out too well, Detective. She and DiNapoli got close, too close for her own safety. I pulled her out on Saturday before the raid at the pier. This traffic is nuts. I'm gonna get out and go through local streets—this traffic sucks."

"Yeah. Good idea, Sarge. We should be at the airport soon. So, this turned out to be a shit storm, didn't it, Sarge?"

"Yeah, Rodriguez, and anybody who knows anything is dead."

"So Sarge, now what, do we just suck it up?"

"What about this guy, Tom? What do we know about him?"

"Tom is above all this, he's a retired officer, served his country and was defending himself against Sanchez and Felix. He fell in love with Anna and he was completely focused on her. Tom was the victim here. Antonio's jealousy almost killed him."

"I get it, Detective."

The car winds though city traffic, making better time than the highway. Rodriguez says, "Looks like we're moving now." The car stops at a light and a truck pulls up to the right side and it catches Rodriguez's eye. It's a carting truck, and the name on the side is DiNapoli Carting. "Look at this, Sarge. Ain't this some shit. Look who's on the right."

McMahon looks out the passenger side window. "Yeah, ain't that some shit. The motherfucker."

The light changes and both vehicles jockey to get ahead of each other. "Let' em go, Sarge. They're bigger than we are. Besides, it would be a shame to bang up a nice new truck." The truck pulls out ahead of their car.

McMahon sees the back of the truck and there it is right above the compactor—the number 82. "Holy shit, Rodriguez! There it is—82 —it's the number of the fucking truck! Son of a bitch! I'm gonna follow it."

"What're you talking about, Sarge?"

"I'll explain later." McMahon follows the truck at a safe distance. "I'd love to see who's driving that truck." They both stop at the next light and the truck is on the right side of the car again. The light changes and the truck moves. Rodriguez grabs the wheel and jerks it to the right hitting the rear of the truck.

McMahon is startled and shouts, "What the hell are you doing?!"

"Stop the car, Sarge! Stop the car—just sit and don't react. Let's see if anybody comes out of the truck."

The truck goes through the intersection and stops. The driver's side door opens and the driver steps out, dressed in a sport jacket and white shirt.

"Does that guy look like he's picking up garbage?"

"Not dressed like that. Let's not spook him. The last thing we need is a 20-ton garbage truck rolling through the streets of Queens at 60 mph."

The man from the truck walks to the back to see what caused the noise. He looks around but doesn't see any damage. He drives on, followed by the car.

"What's with the number 82, Sarge?"

"Ok, Detective, let me give you a quick summary. Cinnamon was supposed to get information on Sanchez. Instead she wound up with DiNapoli."

"What do you mean 'wound up with,' Sarge?"

"DiNapoli saw her dance, gave her his card, and one thing led to another. They wound up sleeping together."

"Shit, talk about taking one for the team."

"It's not what you think, Rodriguez. He never touched her."

"That's hard to believe, Sarge. She's gorgeous."

"Yeah she is, but DiNapoli has issues, Mommy issues—he likes to cuddle. He never touched her, they just cuddled. He talks in his sleep, and he keeps repeating 82 over and over. We couldn't figure it out till now—it's the truck."

"If this is the real deal we should radio for help."

"Yeah, I'll call Ebersole." McMahon calls Ebersole and he picks up. "Hello, McMahon. Are you at the airport?"

"No Captain. Looks like I'm gonna miss my flight. I'm calling for backup."

"That's not funny," Ebersole says.

"I'm serious, Captain, we're following one of DiNapoli's trucks— truck number 82. Don't ask me to explain now, but I think this is what we missed Sunday night." "A carting truck filled with drugs."

"Well, too bad, Sergeant. My men are in the field."

"Not good enough, Captain, we're on Astoria Boulevard Near 101st Street."

"I got nobody. I'm afraid you're on your own."

Rodriguez says, "Put out an 'Officer Needs Assistance' call—he has to respond."

"This is an 'officer needs assistance' call, Captain, you HAVE to help. I'll let you know when we stop moving and I'll give you a location. Get NYPD involved."

Ebersole says, "Dammit, McMahon. Why are you dragging me into this?"

"Cause I wanna make you a hero, Ebersole."

They follow the truck through Queens and they arrive at a desolate section of Long Island City. The area is known for abandoned buildings and old factories. It borders the East River and Brooklyn. The truck turns the corner and stops in front of a large brick building with a sign that reads RDN Importing.

Rodriguez says, "Stop here." The truck's doors open and the men step out and look around.

McMahon says, "I wish I had binoculars. I swear the passenger looks like Dom, DiNapoli's right hand man."

Rodriguez opens the glove compartment and takes out a pair of opera glasses and hands them to McMahon. "Will these do?"

"Opera glasses? What are you doing with opera glasses?"

"I love the opera! 'Carmen' is my favorite ...and he sings, 'Toreador, Toreador.'"

McMahon laughs. "Shut up, Rodriguez, you can't sing for shit. But I'm glad you like opera. It shows you have some culture. I love it, too, but I'm a 'La Boheme girl.'"

McMahon looks through the glasses. "I think we found our shipment. That's definitely Dom." Seconds later the warehouse doors open and a different driver takes the truck inside.

"I gotta get in there—call Ebersole." Rodriguez leaves the car and runs across the street and behind the truck. As the truck enters the warehouse he darts to the right side and hides behind some boxes. McMahon is on the radio with Ebersole. "I need backup now! I'm at 14th Avenue and River Street in Long Island City. The truck is in a warehouse owned by RDN Importing. Rodriguez is inside. Get here quick." Ebersole says, "On the way."

Rodriguez texts McMahon. "The back of the truck just opened. I see crates in the back. I count about 8-10 men, heavily armed. I hope the cavalry is on the way. There's a guy looking at monitors, and there's cameras around the building. I'm gonna get closer to see if I can pull the plug."

McMahon texts back, "Rodriguez—stay put. Ebersole is on the way."

"I can't, Sarge. It's no good if they're spotted. I'm gonna take him out."

Rodriguez slowly comes alongside the man at the console. The fork lift begins unloading the drugs. Rodriguez moves into position using the noise of the machinery to cover his movements. When the opportunity presents itself, he lunges. He grabs the man around the neck and pulls him to the floor. He continues to squeeze cutting off the man's oxygen temporarily rendering him unconscious. He sits at the console and texts McMahon. "All clear."

"Got it!" McMahon answers.

"Where's Ebersole, Sarge? They're unloading now."

"He's on the way. Stay away from the front gates—SWAT's gonna bust through."

Rodriguez moves around the room to get a better position for the element of surprise. Dom is overseeing the unloading with Diego when he spots Rodriguez. Rodriguez doesn't know he was spotted as Dom tells Diego, "I'll get this guy." Dom opens his straight edge Razor and tries to catch Rodriguez off guard. Rodriguez sees him and runs for the stairs to the roof. Dom is in pursuit, razor in hand. Rodriguez gets to the roof and kicks the door open as Dom gets closer. Rodriguez uses the door as a weapon and slams it into Dom as he reaches the roof. Dom pushes it open and the men confront each other. Rodriguez pulls his weapon and tells Dom to drop the razor. "You must be Rodriguez. I heard you're a real hard ass. You think you can take this blade away from me."

"Give it up asshole—troops are on the way. You're done."

"Come on, put your gun down. Let's go one on one. Take my blade, tough guy."

"I'll take it and shove it up your ass. You wanna do this, let's do it." He removes the clip from his weapon and puts his gun on the ground. Dom doesn't hesitate to attack swinging the blade at Rodriguez. He's able to fend off the attack, his jacket protecting his arm. Dom swings at Rodriguez's neck and misses. As he misses, Rodriguez punches him in the face. This stuns Dom and he's getting frustrated, swinging more widely. Dom swings again and catches Rodriguez off guard slashing his right arm. Dom says, "How's that, tough guy?" Dom takes another swing at Rodriguez's stomach and misses, which allows Rodriguez to punch Dom in the face with a series of lefts and right. Dom is reeling and his legs go rubbery. Rodriguez kicks the razor out of Dom's hand. They're now fighting with no weapons mano a mano, and Dom is no match for Rodriguez's strength and youth. Dom realizes he's in trouble and he reaches for his gun thinking Rodriguez is unarmed. Rodriguez falls back and removes his weapon from his ankle holster. He fires two rounds hitting Dom in the chest; he falls back-ward through the skylight to his death three floors below. The NYPD crashes through the front gates and gunfire breaks out, and there's yelling and screaming from below. Rodriguez finds his gun and reloads. His arm is bleeding and he makes a tourniquet to stem the flow.

He slowly makes his way down the stairs. He sees McMahon taking cover behind some boxes and he makes his way over to her. Ebersole and his men are engaged in a fire fight with DiNapoli's men. Rodriguez reaches McMahon and she sees his wound.

"Is that Dom lying there?"

"Yeah, but he got me with his blade."

"Get out of here, Rodriguez. There's some medics outside. They'll treat that wound."

"No, I'm gonna hang with you, Sarge. Somebody's gotta watch your back. Some of DiNapoli's men are beginning to surrender. This is over."

On the balcony above them Diego is taking aim. He fires at Rodriguez and the bullet goes past them and hits the wall behind them. McMahon and Rodriguez look up to the balcony. McMahon recognizes the man.

"Shit, Rodriguez. That's Diego Vargas."

"Who is he?"

"Somebody we need to catch alive. He knows all about Delacruz's operation."

Diego fires again, the bullet ricocheting off the floor near Rodriguez.

"Shit! That was close, Sarge."

"He's Delacruz's business manager. He used to be his enforcer, but he got educated."

"Drug dealers need business managers—who knew?"

McMahon looks at Rodriguez and shakes her head. She gets on the radio to Ebersole. "Captain, that guy on the balcony is Diego Vargas. We need him alive."

Rodriguez says, ``I'm gonna try and get up there. Cover me."

McMahon tells Ebersole, "Rodriguez is going up there. Hold your fire."

Ebersole replies, "I ain't making any promises. He wounded one of my guys, and he's got us pinned down."

"He's Delacruz's money man. We want him alive."

"Like I said McMahon—no promises."

Diego reloads and fires again and yells, "Fuck you, cop."

Rodriguez is on the balcony and getting closer to Diego and he signals to McMahon not to shoot.

He fires again at Ebersole's men. Some of DiNapoli's men have escaped, but those that couldn't have surrendered. McMahon shouts again, "Come on, Diego. You're alone. Drop it and come down."

Diego begins to run across the balcony, firing at both McMahon and Ebersole's men. Agent Harris fires and hits Diego, and he falls—his wound is fatal. McMahon yells "Fuck, I wanted him alive." They run up the stairs to check on his condition.

Agent Harris asks, "Who's this guy?"

"This guy is Delacruz's business manager. We should have taken him alive."

"Business manager—drug dealers need business managers?"

"In 2020 they do. We should have taken him alive."

"Well, McMahon, if somebody's trying to kill me, I kill 'em back. Does Primo ring a bell?"

"Fuck you, Harris."

"Go back to Vegas, McMahon. You're over your head."

Rodriguez runs over and shouts, "Didn't you see me up there, asshole? You could have shot me. I should throw your ass off the balcony."

Harris says, "Anytime, Detective."

Ebersole says, "Walk the fuck away, Harris. Sorry, Sergeant, he was firing at us. He already wounded one of my agents."

The NYPD and Ebersole's men are making arrests and sealing the warehouse.

"Any sign of DiNapoli?" McMahon asks.

"No," replies Ebersole. Rodriguez and McMahon are leaving the warehouse when Ebersole shouts from the warehouse. "Hey, McMahon! My agents just picked up Maxie at the airport."

Rodriguez yells back, "Was he alone?"

"Yeah, Detective. He was alone. No DiNapoli."

# CHAPTER 52

# MAXIE BEHIND BARS

It's been a month since the Sunday night massacre. Rodriguez calls Ebersole to ask if Maxie has cooperated and given any information. Maxie is not cooperating, and Ebersole is no closer to finding DiNapoli, and Delacruz is even further out of reach. Ebersole figures that perhaps Rodriguez may have better luck. Rodriguez arrives at the Suffolk County detention facility. He checks in at the security desk. Ebersole made sure he would be brought in to see Maxie immediately. He's led to a corridor painted institutional green and down the fluorescent lit walkway to a door. He enters. In the room are ten chairs on one side, separated by a plexiglass partition and ten chairs on the other. He sees Maxie waiting for him. He sits down and he notices Maxie is looking tired and drawn. The two men don't talk for a while. Finally Rodriguez breaks the ice. "So, Maxie. How're you feeling?"

"How am I feeling? Are you fucking with me, Sergeant? I'm feeling like I want a bowl of pasta with sauce that doesn't taste like ketchup, a nice plate of broccoli rabe sautéed with garlic, and olive oil washed down with a glass of Chianti and a nice blowjob for dessert. So I guess you're a hero now. I heard you got Fuller's spot. Fucking Fuller. I'm glad he's dead, the pedophile prick. So what brings you to see me, Sergeant? Are you here to make a deal? Ebersole tried and I told him to go fuck himself. Unless your deal cuts me loose and all is forgiven you can fuck off, too."

Rodriguez let Maxie talk—now he asks: "Are you ok in here? Is anybody fucking with you, Maxie?"

"Thanks for asking, but I got two things working for me here. Nobody wants to fuck an old nerd like me, and the jerkoffs in this place know I'm with Richie DiNapoli's crew. No, Sergeant. I don't need shit from you."

"Hey, DiNapoli's crew left town. You're alone pal, the old gang is dead."

"It's a temporary thing, Rodriguez. Don't sell Richie short—he'll be back. In the meantime his money is safe cause I'm the only one who knows where it is."

"So Maxie, where do you think Richie is right now? Costa Rica? Somewhere in South America? Maybe he's with Delacruz, eating lobster and banging Colombian chicks. Columbian women are beautiful, aren't they, Maxie? What do you think?"

"I think you're trying to fuck with my head, Sergeant. You know, turn me against Richie. Let me tell you something you cops don't understand. It's called loyalty. Richie's been more than a boss to the family—he's been a dear friend for many years."

"So what do you expect him to do, Rodriguez? Walk in here with his hands in the air and say 'I'm here. Lock me up?'"

"If the situation were reversed, I'd do the same thing—bide my time and when the time was right start up again somewhere else. Yeah, Richie will be back, Sergeant. Now let me ask you something. Do you think this case is solved and closed? Most of DiNapoli's crew are either hiding or in jail. You can't touch them. Delacruz, he's protected by crooked cops and politicians south of the border. Now be honest with yourself—do you really think the mastermind behind this was Antonio Sanchez?"

"No, it was Diego Vargas."

"Well, you're right about one thing—Sanchez was a loose cannon dumb spic who couldn't mastermind a circle jerk. That leads us to Diego Vargas. Now I agree that he's got ten times more smarts than Sanchez - you know, cool, collected, rational - but he was in Colombia setting this up down there. No, Sergeant, I'm talking about here in New York and Long Island. Come to think of it, you stumbled your way through this case."

"What're you talking about, Maxie?"

"Well Rodriguez, for starters you didn't get DiNapoli, Delacruz is untouchable unless the CIA sends in a hit squad, which ain't gonna happen, and you took a detour on your way to the airport and found the drugs. I read all about it in the papers. I think you need to resume your search for the person pulling the strings, catch that person and you'll redeem yourself as a detective—just saying. Come back and let me know how you make out."

"Why are you so interested in this mastermind, Maxie? Is there something you wanna tell me."

"No Sergeant. What I know I'll take to the grave. It's dinner time. I gotta go and eat some slop."

———

Rodriguez is driving back to Oceanview with Maxie's words playing over and over in his head. He calls McMahon and she answers. "Hello, Sergeant Rodriguez. I believe congratulations are in order. We're peers now. How's it feel, Sergeant?"

"It feels great, but you know you'll always be my boss. So guess who I saw today."

"Who?"

"Maxie. He and I had a long talk."

"Did he give anything up?"

"No, he said he's never gonna give Richie up. He also said something that got me thinking. He said we never found out who the mastermind was behind this deal. He told me this person is still out there."

"Did it occur to you that he was messing with your head?"

"Yeah, it did, but he made his point, and now I'm thinking about what he said."

"Listen, Rodriguez. The opinion of everybody involved was that the brain behind this was Diego Vargas. But I get the feeling that's not good enough for you, is it? So what do you want to do about it, Rodriguez?"

"I want to keep digging. This thing is beginning to eat at me. I may need your help."

"You've always had good instincts, Rodriguez. How can I help?"

"Thanks, McMahon. Can you send me all you got on Delacruz?"

"That's a lot of material. How far back do you want to go?"

"I'll take whatever you got."

"Ok, Rodriguez, but it's gonna take awhile."

"It's ok. I'm gonna stop by and see how Tom's doing, so I'll be away from the precinct for a few hours. Thanks, Sarge. We'll talk later."

# CHAPTER 53

# WHY OCEANVIEW?

Rodriguez arrives at Tom's house and is welcomed by Anna, and she invites him in. Tom is sitting on the couch reading a book. He greets Rodriguez. "Congratulations, Sergeant! Nice of you to stop by. I'd like you to meet Anna."

Anna extends her hands and says, "Nice to finally meet you, Sergeant. Thank you for everything you've done for us."

"You're welcome, Anna. I was just doing my job. So Tom, how are you feeling?"

"Today is not so bad, but it can change when the headaches get bad. I get vertigo, my vision blurs, and what's worse is, it can happen anytime. What bothers me the most is I'm still not cleared to fly."

"That's too bad, Tom. I know how much you love it."

Anna asks, "Are you going to stay a while, Sergeant? Have a seat and I'll make some coffee."

Rodriguez says, "Is it ok if I ask you a few questions about that night, Tom? Is it ok, Anna? I know Antonio was your husband."

Anna replies, "Do you need me for this? I was about to run some errands."

"No, it's ok Anna. Go ahead. I just have a few loose ends to straighten out."

Rodriguez helps Anna with her coat. He extends his hands and says, "Very nice to meet you, Anna. I hope to see you again."

"Nice meeting you also, Sergeant. Goodbye."

Anna says to Tom, "I'll be in town. If you need me, just call. Ok, Baby?" She kisses Tom and leaves.

Rodriguez says, "So Tom, now that Anna's not here, why do you think Sanchez wanted you dead?"

"I think you know the answer, Sergeant. We were having an affair."

"Yeah, I heard about Antonio's insane jealousy. How much do you know about what happened that night?"

"Just what I read in the papers, Sergeant."

"Did you ever suspect Sanchez was involved in something this big, from a cop's perspective?"

"No, I knew he was a scumbag, but I thought he was a nickel and dime scumbag. But from what I read it was quite a score."

"Cut the right way, the street value could be fifty million to seventy million. That's a conservative estimate. In the right hands it could go for ten to twenty million more."

"I know DiNapoli got away. Any idea where he is, Sergeant?"

"No, we got people working on it. It seems like he fell off the face of the earth."

"And the cartel in Colombia—any word on Delacruz?"

"I'm afraid he's gonna be a lot tougher to find. You know, Tom, everybody's getting paid, crooked cops, politicians—they keep him insulated. Let me be honest with you, Tom. I'm not convinced that it's over. I think there's still a part of this that's not finished. Do you think Sanchez was smart enough to put something this big together?"

Tom laughs, and Rodríguez laughs along with him. "You wanna know what I think, Sergeant? I think Colombia was pulling the strings." "Yeah, Tom, I agree. I think Sanchez was taking orders from Medellin."

"So Sergeant, what brought you to Oceanview? What's the real story?"

Rodriguez thinks about the question for a while and he answers: "I was with the Las Vegas DEA for about eight years. My commanding officer was Sergeant Elizabeth McMahon, and being in law enforcement, Tom, I'm sure you've had some tough commanders. Well, McMahon is someone you don't want to get into a pissing contest with. She'll slap your dumb ass around real quick. She and I worked many cases together, including this one. So back to your original question. About six months ago a journalist friend of mine called me and told me he had documents that showed a certain middle eastern royal family was supplying weapons to terrorists. He gave me the documents and I contacted the consulate. I told them I had this evidence, and I wanted two hundred thousand dollars for it.

"Shit, Sergeant—you were blackmailing them?"

"Yeah, in the technical sense, but I wasn't gonna keep the money— it was going to a good cause."

"Good cause? What good cause?"

"I'm gonna tell you something, Tom, that nobody knows. Not even McMahon, who I'm very close to. I'm a twin. My sister was born with a rare childhood disease that affects the nervous system. There's no cure, but it's being worked on. The only thing missing is money. That was the plan—the two hundred grand was going to the scientists trying to find a cure. We were making the exchange at a hotel parking lot in Vegas when things went south. We were changing the money for the documents when one of the assholes asked me if those were the only copies, so of course, being a smartass I said maybe."

"Shit Rodriguez—what happened when you said that?"

"Well, these guys obviously had no sense of humor and they tried to kill me."

Both men laugh, then Rodriguez added, "I regret that I had to go outside the line that I drew for myself, but I'm desperate to help my sister. She's incapable of doing anything for herself because of this disease. Two people died that night and two were wounded. I knew going in that no matter what I did these guys were gonna kill me. A few days later McMahon sent me to Oceanview to keep an eye on Sanchez. A couple of these guys had State Department ID's so it became an international incident. I know McMahon was protecting me by sending me here to work on this case. She's still dealing with the fallout, and you'll never see this on the news because it's being covered up. I know there's things going on behind the scenes—you know, investigations and all that shit, but the public will never know about it. I'm not proud of what happened that night, somebody died, but I would do it again. There was no money, the whole thing was a set up. They were going to get the documents and kill me. So that's my story." Rodriguez looks at his watch and adds, "Damn, time flies. I gotta take off, Tom. My crew will be wondering where I am."

"Ok, Rodriguez, come back soon. Next time we'll have something stronger than coffee."

"Sounds good. Give my regards to Anna. You're a lucky man to have her by your side."

"I know, thanks. Bye, Sergeant." Tom closes the door and sits on the couch. He puts his head back and closes his eyes.

# CHAPTER 54
# THE MASTERMIND

Anna is walking on Gold Street in the city of Oceanview. Gold Street is the Rodeo Drive of Oceanview with high end boutiques lining both sides of the street. She's been shopping most of the afternoon at some of these boutiques - boutiques like Gucci, Versace, and Ferragamo. Get the picture? Her phone rings and it's a number she doesn't recognize, but it has an international area code and she answers "Hola!"

The voice on the other end says, "Hola, mi corazon."

"Tio, how are you? I've been worried about you."

"Don't worry about me, my darling. Can you talk?"

"Yes, I'm out shopping. Tom is home. I feel so bad for him. He's still getting those headaches."

"That's too bad. How is he treating you, my dear?"

"Tom is wonderful, Tio. He's a good man."

"I wish I could've gotten my hands on that pendejo Sanchez. I would have fed him to my dogs. Every day I would think about the way he was treating you—that piece of shit."

"Tio, be careful. You always tell me someone might be listening."

"Perhaps, but not on this phone. You see, I have a friend in the C.I.A.—his daughter needs braces to straighten her crooked gringo teeth so when she grows up she won't be so ugly. So I traded him his daughter's perfect smile for a phone that can't be traced. I paid for her braces, that's how things are done down here, clean and simple."

"You make me laugh, Tio."

"Well it's true, cara mia, he had something that I needed, and I had something he needed. See, simple - like I said."

"Now tell me about Tom. Do you love him."

"Yes I do, Tio. I've never felt this way about any man before."

"Tell me about him."

"Well, he's a war hero from the Gulf War, and he's got medals for saving his men under fire. He's a retired policeman."

"A policeman, how ironic. Go ahead. Continue."

"He has a plane and it's beautiful. It's red and white. I went flying with him. It was wonderful. I felt so free."

"What does he know about our business, about us?"

"Nothing Tio. I would never tell him. Do you think I would reveal what we do?"

"No, no, never. But let me ask you a question. Do you feel that he would ever want to join our family?"

"Family, you mean marriage?"

The voice laughs. "Marriage? You are in love! No, no. I'm speaking of the business."

"No Tio, not Tom. He's too honest. He would never break the law."

"I see—so we have a decorated war hero, a policeman who's honest and can't be persuaded to join our family. That's a dilemma, my darling."

"A dilemma? Why, Tio?"

"It's a dilemma because, for instance—and this is just a 'for instance'—if he were to find out about our business, what are you prepared to do?"

Anna stops in front of a Gucci store to admire a pair of shoes. The voice continues: "You haven't answered my question, my darling niece."

"Tio, you know family comes first, I'd have to kill him. I have to go. I just saw the most wonderful pair of shoes that I must have."

"Wait, before you go. I just want you to know that not a minute goes by when I'm not thinking of your brother Diego."

"I know, Tio, me too."

"One day we 'll have our revenge but I can't move freely now. The policia and their counterparts from America are watching. I'll be in touch, my dear. Adios."

# CHAPTER 55

# THE FACEOFF

Rodriguez is back at the precinct, and as he walks to his office, his men hand him phone messages. He quickly reads through the messages and he stops at a message from Mrs. Cooper. He goes into his office and throws the messages on his desk. He sits at his computer to see what McMahon sent him. The files paint a picture of Delacruz as a strong member of the community, whether it's receiving an Award for charity work, golfing with politicians and precinct captains or building a church. Rodriguez continues going through the file on Delacruz. He's convinced there's some things in the files he's missing.

Tom awakens from his nap and calls for Anna. He goes, to the kitchen looking for a snack. He says to himself that if she's not home in a half hour he'll call to make sure she's ok. He's getting bored and he begins to wander the house. He's always respected Anna's privacy, but now the detective in him is taking over. Next to the master bedroom in the rear of the house there's a room he's never seen. The door is always locked, and he felt it would be a betrayal of trust to even ask about it. He feels around the top of the door frame for a key. As he enters the room he notices that like the rest of the house it's beautifully decorated. It's very masculine—a cross between an office and a man-cave. On the wall is a wide screen TV opposite a queen size sofa. The walls are painted a forest green with baseball memorabilia on display. Some of the items could be worth thousands of dollars, not bad for someone who doesn't have a steady job. A beautiful antique bookcase occupies half a wall. It's filled with books, and as Tom gets closer, he notices that some of the books are collectables. He sees that Rebecca's books about stained glass are on the book shelf, and he wonders why Anna would lock them in a room. Tom sees a book that seems out of place—it's a copy of The Bible. He finds it strange that this book would be among the others since Anna never discussed religion or had never gone to a house of worship since they've been together. He notices a white piece of paper, perhaps a bookmark, protruding from the center of the book. He takes the book off the shelf and removes the folded piece of paper. He slowly unfolds the paper and is shocked to find a certificate of confirmation for a Mercedes Delacruz. His heart is racing as he continues to look through the book. Nestled between the pages toward the back of the book he finds a photograph of a young girl of about fourteen years old and a boy of about twelve. They are standing with an older man, a rather unattractive man. The young girl is wearing a white dress with a tiara. In her right hands is a book that looks a lot like the bible he's holding. Tom is thinking that there's a rational explanation for it. His love for Anna is clouding his logic. He plays various scenarios over in his head but a closer examination confirms that it's Anna. He puts the certificate and the photograph in his pocket. He places the book back on the shelf in the same position and leaves the room. He locks the door and puts the key back on the door frame.

Rodriguez is at his desk going through the files McMahon sent him. He glances at the message from Mrs. Cooper and dreads calling her. He's been occupied with the drug trafficking case and hasn't devoted the time to continue the investigation into the disappearance of Evelyn Lynch. He's positive she was murdered by Sanchez and Felix, but he needs to find the remains so her grandmother has closure. He plays over in his head what he's going to say to her.

Tom is pacing the living room. He's experiencing many different emotions. He wonders how she could have deceived him for a long time and how he was so in love not to see through the charade. He decides to end the masquerade and calls Rodriguez, knowing full well he'll never be with Anna.

Rodriguez is ready to call Mrs. Cooper; he realizes he has to walk a fine line and not reveal too much but, at the same time not to squash her hope. He knows the fragile state she's in, and besides, nobody wants to hear that their granddaughter is dead over the phone. He picks up his phone reluctantly to call Mrs. Cooper. As he's about to dial, a call comes through and it's Tom. Rodriguez feels a little relief and he answers. "Hi, Tom. Is everything ok?"

"No Sergeant, I don't think so. I may have found our mastermind. Does the name Mercedes Delacruz mean anything to you? I found a certificate of Confirmation with her name and a photograph of a man with two children. One of the children looks like Anna. She's dressed in a white dress. You know, a Confirmation dress.

Rodriguez says, "Damn, is Anna in the house?"

"No, she's out but she may be back soon."

"Tom, you have to be one hundred percent sure."

"I'm sure it's Anna, and the certificate is signed by Jorge Delacruz as her guardian." Tom still has his back to the door and didn't hear Anna come in. She's heard part of the conversation and she moves closer to Tom, who's still not aware that she's back. Tom says to Rodriguez, "There's a boy in the picture. Do you have any idea who that might be?"

"No I don't."

Anna has a gun at her side; she lifts it and puts it to the back of Tom's neck. Tom feels the cold metal and he slowly turns and sees Anna. She signals to him to end the call. Tom says to Rodriguez, "Ok, McMahon, I gotta go now. We'll talk later."

Anna asks Tom, "Who the fuck is McMahon?"

"It's Rodriguez's boss."

"How did you figure it out?"

Tom holds up the picture and the certificate. Anna looks at the picture and she points to it with the gun. "The boy, you wanna know who he is? It's my brother, Diego Delacruz. Of course, he changed his name to Diego Vargas so he wouldn't be hunted like a dog. Your pig friends killed him, Tom."

"I had nothing to do with that."

"You're a cop, you're all the same."

Rodriguez says to himself, "McMahon? What the fuck was he talking about?" He keeps scrolling on the computer until he comes across the same picture that Tom found. This picture was in El Colombiano, a local newspaper in Medellin. The caption reads "Jorge Delacruz, a philanthropist and a resident of Medellin, at the Confirmation of his niece Mercedes Delacruz at the Church of Our Lady of Miracles, the church he had built through his generosity." Rodriguez stops reading, grabs his jacket and bolts out of his office. He shouts to Detective Spinelli, "Spinelli you're in charge till I get back." Rodriguez jumps into his car and turns on the lights and sirens.

Anna says to Tom, "Move. Let's go to the car."

"You gonna kill me, Anna? Go ahead. Do it here, or are you afraid to get blood all over your designer couch?"

"Move, Tom, I'm serious. Get in the car."

Tom knows he has to stall, the precinct is ten minutes away. He's hoping that Rodriguez realized that something is wrong. He says to Anna, "I guess all that talk about loving me was bullshit, wasn't it, Anna?"

"Family comes first, Tom. I was praying you wouldn't find out. But now you leave me no choice. Go to the car Tom. Now."

He begins to walk to the car when Anna asks, "Where's your gun?" He points to the table by the couch but he's wearing his ankle holster with a loaded gun. He puts his hands in the air and says, "Do you wanna search me?"

"Keep walking and go to the car."

Rodriguez is a few blocks away—he turns off his lights and siren and turns onto Tom and Anna's street. He sees Anna and Tom getting into the car. Anna still has the gun pointed at Tom's back. "So where do you plan on killing me, Anna?"

"Drive, Tom, and shut your fucking mouth."

Tom looks in his rear view mirror and sees a black sedan parked behind them.

"I need air, Anna. Can I roll down the window?"

"I don't give a fuck, Tom. Just drive or I'll kill you here in the car."

Tom rolls down the window and begins to drive. He looks in the rear view mirror and sees the black sedan driving behind them. He puts his hand outside the window and signals to Rodriguez. Tom is waiting for the opportunity to pull the gun in his ankle holster. The car is driving down an isolated dirt road near the Oceanview city dump. They drive a half mile and stop at a secluded area with tall grass and rusted hulks of cars that were dumped there years ago. Anna tells Tom, "Get out and start walking towards the water." Rodriguez stopped his car and he's using the tall grass as cover as he's heading towards them, gun in hand. They walk down a small pathway to the water. To the right there's an abandoned ranger station. Rodriguez is about fifty feet away, hiding in the reeds. He continues to move inch by inch closer to them. "Get into the house Tom. Move!"

"Was this planned all along, just in case I found out?"

"Move, Tom. Get inside and shut up. Don't make this tougher than it is."

Rodriguez realizes now is the time to make his move. He runs toward Anna and screams, "Drop your weapon and don't move!"

Anna turns and fires at Rodriguez. Her first shot grazes Rodriguez in the leg. He returns fire and hits Anna. The wound is not serious and Anna turns her gun on Tom. Tom used the distraction to pull the gun from his ankle holster. Tom is facing Anna and both have guns drawn. Tom says, "Drop it, Anna. Don't make me shoot you."

Anna is bleeding from her arm. "Look what this fucking pig did to me, Tom. Kill him."

Rodriguez comes out of the tall grass. He tells Anna, "You can only kill one of us, Anna."

Anna says to Tom, "Go ahead, Tom. Kill him. We can be together forever. There's money, Tom, more than you can imagine. We can live the life people dream of. We can go to Colombia. My uncle will protect us."

Tom turns his weapon on Rodriguez and he says, "Sorry pal. I love her."

Rodriguez says, "You're not going to kill me, Tom. She was behind this whole drug deal. Tom, do you think she gives a shit about you? It's family first, Tom. You know how it is."

Tom drops his weapon and says, "Go ahead, Anna. Kill me."

Anna says, "What the fuck are you doing, Tom?"

"I knew you couldn't shoot me, it's between you and Rodriguez now."

Rodriguez still has his gun trained on Anna. He says, "Come on, Mercedes. It's over. Drop it. No me hagas Matarte."

"Don't speak Spanish to me! You're not one of us. You're a fucking gringo cop."

"What's it gonna be, Mercedes?"

Tom says, "Drop it Anna. You know he'll kill you if you don't."

Anna looks at Tom and back at Rodriguez and drops her weapon. Rodriguez moves in and cuffs Anna. He calls for backup and an ambulance for him and Anna; they're taken away to the hospital for medical attention. Tom is taken back to the house he shared with Rebecca.

# CHAPTER 56

# DELACRUZ'S DRONES

Jorge Delacruz is seated at a table with seven of his closest associates. He's anxiously smoking a cigar and mumbling to himself. He suspiciously looks around the table at the men gathered there. The associates sense this and nervously glance at each other. His manservant brings newspapers and a beautifully carved ornate box. Delacruz tells his manservant to "put the box here." And he points to the table directly in front of him. He looks around the table and he speaks to his manservant. "Give them the newspaper—one for each." The manservant distributes the papers, the men glancing at each other. Delacruz takes a long drag on his cigar and throws it on the ground. He opens the box and takes out a silver-plated 357 magnum. He places it on the table in front of him. In one motion he sweeps the box off the table and it crashes to the floor with a thud, and the men jump in their seats at the sound.

"This gun was given to me by the Medellin Chief of Police. See? Here on the handle, it's engraved. Ironic, isn't it?"

'I keep it loaded, but I've never used it."

Delacruz speaks to the man on his right. "Read the headline out loud so we all can hear."

The man begins to read slowly his voice unsteady: "Mercedes Delacruz, the niece of Jorge Delacruz, was arrested in New York on drug trafficking charges and attempted murder."

Delacruz says, "Enough." He points to the next man and says, "You read it."

This continues around the table until Delacruz asks, "Was I betrayed by one or all of you? I don't sleep at night. I think of my nephew Diego, who was more man than all of you. My niece, my dear niece, in some fucking gringo prison. I'm being watched. Sometimes I hear the drones, I hear the helicopters. Why do I pay you fucking people? Isn't it your job to protect me and my family from these fucking gringos?" They look nervously around the table. Delacruz looks up at the sky and adds: "Look at them—flying around like little fucking mosquitos." He smacks his arm for effect. "See, I just killed one." He continues to look at the sky. "I have merchandise I can't move because I'm being watched. I can't touch my money. I'm being isolated from the rest of the world. Listen, listen to the drones buzzing around above us." The men look up at the sky and at each other.

The man to his left says, "Padrone, there's no drones above us." Delacruz looks at the man for a while and he says, "You don't see the drones?" He picks up the magnum and shoots the man in the chest. The man is wide-eyed and shocked and he sputters, "Padrone, you shot me!"

"Yes I know. Do you see the drones now, pendejo?" He fires again and again and throws the weapon down on the table. "The rest of you—bury him in the jungle and get the fuck off my land."

# CHAPTER 57

# EVELYN LYNCH FOUND

For the next two weeks the media is abuzz with the story. Rodriguez is in his office filling out reports and closing the file on the case. He's almost completely recovered from his gunshot wound. He's ready to leave for the day when his phone rings and he answers, "This is Sergeant Rodriguez."

The voice asks, "How's the leg?"

He sits back down at his desk and says, "Who's this?"

"It's Maxie. Why don't you take a ride and come see me tomorrow? We'll chat."

"About what? I thought we already had our chat. Listen, Maxie, the next time I talk to you is when you start giving me information, and how the fuck did you get my number?"

"I told you Richie still has pull in this joint. "Don't worry about where I got it, come see me tomorrow in the afternoon around three —I got something for you."

Maxie disconnects the call. Rodriguez gets to the prison at 2:45; the guards at the processing desk usher him in and take him straight to Maxie.

"Hi Rodriguez, how's tricks? I see you still got a little limp."

"Yeah, but it's getting better. What do you want?"

Maxie leans back in his chair and lets out a sigh. He leans forward again so no one else can hear. "Remember the last time you were here, I told you I would never give Richie up. Well, that hasn't changed, but what I will do is tell you how I used to skim Richie's money right off the top."

"You were stealing from Richie? Why are you telling me this?"

"Because I like you, Sergeant. You're trying to do the right thing. We don't have to hate each other. Do you wanna hear more?"

"Yeah. Go ahead, Maxie."

"Before I continue, you gotta promise me one thing—this doesn't go any further than right here."

"Go ahead, Maxie. It won't go anywhere."

"Like I told you before, I was always loyal to Richie, but I felt I wanted a little piece of the action. Now don't get me wrong, Sergeant. Richie took good care of his crew. I have been handling Richie's money for twenty years. You know, shell companies, offshore accounts, moving money around and making sure his money grows. Did you know some of these accounts pay interest on your money?"

"I know, some more than others."

"That's where I skimmed, on the interest. It worked like this—if the account paid 4% interest I'd have 2% sent to my account in the same bank under a shell company. Now, you're thinking to yourself, 'what's 2%,' right? Well, I'll tell you, after twenty years of two, three or more percent, I've accumulated millions."

"Shit, Maxie. Weren't you afraid Richie would find out."

"Nah. As long as his money was steady or growing, he was alright. In dealing with these banks I found out one thing, everybody has a price, even bank presidents. When Richie started this deal with Delacruz he deposited twenty million dollars in ten different accounts. In order to do that I had to have Delacruz's account numbers. I had to pay off a lot of bank presidents to get access to Delacruz's accounts."

"Goddamn, Maxie. You must have a death wish. Did you ever think what would happen if Delacruz found out?"

"Not really. You see, every time there was a movement on Delacruz's accounts, money out or money in, I would get a notification on my phone. All under the radar. I wasn't able to touch the money, but I got an activity report for every transaction. Once it was set up, it was on cruise control. If I told you how much that cocksucker Delacruz had in these accounts your head will explode." At that moment the bell rings, signaling the end of visiting hours. Maxie added, "What if I told you that I knew who the mastermind was months ago? I figured it out by following the money. Shit, I hate clichés, but it's true."

"How did you figure it out?"

"Next time you visit I'll tell you about it. Now I got something for you, Rodriguez. You got a pen and paper?" The guard walks over to remind the men it's time to go. Rodriguez flashes his badge and the guard says, "Ok, Sergeant. Five minutes." Rodriguez takes out a pen and paper and is ready to write.

Maxie says, "Santangelo Salvage on Dock Street in Oceanview, down by the water. Sanchez and some prick named Felix dumped a body there."

"How do you know that, Maxie?"

"While we were putting this deal together, Richie didn't trust Sanchez so he had him followed. We had a sit down at the social club in Brooklyn and Richie confronted that fucking Sanchez. He admitted to dumping the body in the salvage yard. The way Sanchez told it, Felix and the stripper.... "

Rodriguez cuts him off. "The stripper has a name, Maxie. It's Evelyn Lynch."

"Yeah, that's right. Sanchez said Evelyn was her name. How did you know, Sergeant?"

"I know because it was my case. I saw Sanchez and Felix dump the body in a car trunk on surveillance video. Thanks for helping me close the case, Maxie. I appreciate it. You didn't have to tell me shit."

"Like I said, Sergeant. You're doing the right thing. Come back soon. We'll chat some more."

---

Evelyn Lynch's body was found four days after the visit with Maxie. She was discarded like the rusted and dented skeletons of cars on death row, in line to be crushed and turned to liquid metal. Rodriguez was on the scene when her remains were found. One would never accuse Rodriguez of being sensitive, but the way life ended for Evelyn brought a tear to his eye. A girl who made bad life choices and wound up a victim to a lowlife drug addict. Rodriguez thinks to himself at least the grandmother will have closure now.

# EPILOGUE

This was the first installment in the Rodriguez trilogy. In the second installment his courage and investigative instincts will be put to the test when he encounters the most diabolical and monstrous nemesis in The Cyclist Club.

Who or what will Sergeant Rodriguez confront in the third installment of the Rodriguez Trilogy? Coming soon…

# ABOUT THE AUTHOR

George Marzocchi has authored the crime novel Stained Glass and two more sequels to come in the Detective Rodriguez Trilogy. He began writing with an eye toward crime and fictional detective genres.

George is an avid fan of cinematography and classic/nouveau film noir. He has a visual eye and he has spent many years as a professional photographer and is currently working in the large graphics display field.

George has a love of travel and recently enjoyed trips to Sardinia, Rome, Italy, Bruges Ghent, Antwerp, Paris and Cologne, Germany (taking photos throughout).

He studied photography and visual design at the New School in New York City. He resides in both Manhattan, New York, and Milford, Connecticut with his wife Terry and their two cats, Caribou Cody and Balkie.

He is the proud father of Damien and Julian.

George loves gardening, photography, cooking and tennis.